"Leave your shoes on...for me," Dax murmured

Chloe noted the gleam in his eyes as he spoke...a gleam she liked. "I think that can be arranged," she said.

She kissed him then, with a passion and a need she'd never felt before. She wanted Dax even if it was only for one night.

His arms tightened around her waist and then he slowly eased the zipper down her back. A moment later the dress puddled at her feet and she stood before him clad in the finest silver garter belt, stockings and bra.

"If I'd known you were wearing silver...to match those shoes." He grinned wickedly. "Well, I'd have pulled you into the back room and made love to you on the poker table hours ago."

Chloe shivered. "So you approve?"

"Very much." And with that Dax swept her into his arms, carrying her—shoes and all—into the bedroom.

Dear Reader,

Welcome to The Cowboy Club! This legendary bar/
restaurant is located in colorful Red Rock, Colorado.
Locals consider The Cowboy Club the heart and soul of
the town. Nearly everyone has a story to tell about the
place. And *everybody* has met somebody special there....

Step into The Cowboy Club and take a seat. Experience
the magic of this romantic place. Watch as strong, sexy
heroes encounter the kind of sassy women that make
them want to give up their bachelor ways and commit.

In *The Bride Wore Boots,* Manhattan shoe designer
Chloe James has inherited half of the club. She's
determined to sell out in a "New York minute." Until she
falls into the arms of Dax Charboneau. This sexy bad boy
is her new partner—and he's got plans for Chloe *and* the
club!

Come back to the club in July 1999, with #737 *The Baby
and the Cowboy.* Wiley Cooper falls in love when
gorgeous lawyer Jessica Kilmer comes to town. But their
relationship takes a new twist when someone abandons a
baby at The Cowboy Club...and Jessica gets temporary
custody.

Hope you enjoy your visit to The Cowboy Club!

Happy reading,

Janice Kaiser

THE BRIDE WORE BOOTS
Janice Kaiser

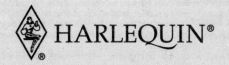

TORONTO • NEW YORK • LONDON
AMSTERDAM • PARIS • SYDNEY • HAMBURG
STOCKHOLM • ATHENS • TOKYO • MILAN • MADRID
PRAGUE • WARSAW • BUDAPEST • AUCKLAND

For Linda Duckett,
who loves shoes as much as I do....
And for our memories of
the pink toe shoes.

ISBN 0-373-25814-3

THE BRIDE WORE BOOTS

Copyright © 1999 by Belles Lettres, Inc.

1

"OH MY GOD, Chloe, you've outdone yourself this time. These are the most beautiful shoes I've ever seen in my life. They'll be absolutely perfect for my dress." There was a tear in Belinda's eye as she held up the shoes for everyone to see.

Chloe James was pleased, even though her stomach was churning with anxiety. That call from her banker couldn't have come at a worse time, when she was in a hurry to leave her shop and meet her friends. Still, this was always her favorite moment—when someone she knew got her first glimpse of the wedding shoes Chloe had made. The first time she'd designed shoes for a member of the Thursday Night Club had been when Liz Cabot and Colby Sommers had married on Valentine's Day. Liz had worn red, and Chloe had made sensational red satin pumps to go with the dress. Because Liz was tiny and Colby was a typical Texan, tall and sexy and all male, the shoes had had a slight platform, and Chloe had done some lovely garnet beadwork across the toe.

Yes, it was far better to think about making her friends happy than to dwell on her financial problems. Chloe looked at the smiling faces around the table, telling herself this was what truly mattered—sharing and giving. She took a deep breath, forcing herself to think about the others she'd favored with a special pair of shoes, the women from the Thursday

Night Club for Divorcées, Spinsters and Other Reprobates who had gone on to exchange the single life for one with a man.

After Liz, the next bride in the group had been Pam Wilson. Though it was her first marriage, Pam had opted for a pale blue suit when she'd wed fellow lawyer Grayson Bartholomew. Chloe had designed T-strap heels for Pam. They'd been made out of the softest kid available and dyed to exactly match her suit.

Now it was Belinda's turn to be the bride, which also meant this would be her last meeting with the Thursday Night Club. The rules were, once you were engaged, you could attend a final meeting in the hope that you might come to your senses. If you were still determined to wed after that, then you were out of the club. None of the six women who had formed the group four years earlier were still members—they'd all gone on to wedded bliss.

Jane Martin, one of the founders, had been head of marketing for the Clairbourne Hotel in midtown New York, and she'd been responsible for getting them a terrific rate on the smallest meeting room in the lower level of the hotel. The food was good there and the price couldn't be beaten, though with its low ceilings and white walls, the room was uninspired.

For special occasions, like Christmas and Valentine's Day, they decorated the meeting room themselves. And they really went all out when one of their members was leaving. Tonight there were balloons tied to the back of Belinda's chair and crepe-paper wedding bells hung from the ceiling over the center of the table. There was even a small floral arrangement.

Belinda Nelson, a tall and willowy book editor

whose natural pale blond hair made her the envy of everyone, was the latest defector. She was engaged to Charles Hoffmann, a famous English mystery writer. Everyone had brought an engagement gift, most of them joke presents. But in keeping with recent tradition, the last present—and the only serious gift—was Chloe's.

Sharon Walton took the box from Belinda's hand and picked up one of the shoes. It had a three-inch heel and was made of a rich cream satin. But what made the shoe really stand out was the thin Austrian-crystal ankle strap. It was perfectly plain and, by the look of awe on Sharon's face, the most elegant thing she had ever seen.

"You know, I could sell these for over four hundred dollars any day of the week."

Sharon, a brunette with chocolate eyes to match her hair, was a personal shopper at Bergdorf's, and knew what she was talking about. She had pleaded with Chloe to go into mass-production, knowing that was the only sure way her company could make it big. But Chloe's dream had been to design and make one-of-a-kind shoes, so she'd steadfastly resisted the idea.

Ariel Johnson reached over and took the satin shoe from Sharon, holding it up to the light. "Belinda's right. You have outdone yourself this time, Chloe. It almost makes me wish I was the one getting married."

"That'll be the day," Wendy Goldstein said. "You and I will be the last two holdouts."

"Oh yeah. What about me?" Angela Cavioli, a senior accountant for one of the big seven, and probably the most outrageous of the group—though Wendy gave her a lot of competition—regarded each of her friends in turn. "I've been around just as long as you, Wendy, and a couple of months longer than Ariel." Angela paused dramatically to let the weight of that pronouncement sink in. "And, as resident expert, I predict that Ariel will be the next to go. God knows, with her looks, she gets the most dates."

Ariel was a former model and, with her pale cocoa skin and long elegant limbs, she was a stunner. Nowadays she ran a modeling agency. She was known for turning down more dates in a week than any two or three of the other women in the group would have had in six months.

"Forget it, girlfriend. I am committed to the single life," Ariel said. "C-o-m-m-i-t-t-e-d. Chloe won't be designing shoes for this girl's trip down the aisle... unless it's as a bridesmaid."

Everyone laughed.

"That could be arranged," Chloe said with a chuckle. Then, in spite of her resolve not to sound maudlin, she couldn't keep a catch out of her voice. "Assuming I'm still in business, of course."

Ariel immediately put down the shoe and took Chloe's hand. "Don't tell me you didn't get the loan."

"All right, I won't tell you."

Belinda groaned. "What are you going to do?"

Chloe unconsciously ran her fingers back through her short black curly hair. With a French mother who worked for one of New York's leading fashion designers as a head seamstress, and an Irish father who owned a neighborhood shoe repair shop in Queens, designing shoes had been a natural. Chloe had the chic of her mother, was always superbly groomed, and her clear Irish skin and emerald green eyes gave her an exotic look.

Over the past six years, she'd built up a reputation as the woman to go to if you wanted a very special pair of shoes—and didn't mind paying hundreds of dollars for the privilege. She'd designed and made shoes for film stars, socialites and even members of Britain's royal family.

But though her clients paid top dollar for her shoes and sandals and boots, Chloe had had trouble making ends meet since she had bought out her partner the year before. Marcus had started the company with her, and he had handled the marketing end of the business. Like Sharon, he'd insisted that if the company was to grow, they should mass-produce. He and Chloe had often argued about it.

She'd given in once, at least to the extent of doing several thousand dollars' worth of shoes on spec. That deal had turned sour in more ways than one. Despite that, Marcus had continued to argue that the company should go one way, while she remained adamant that it go another. Finally, things had come to a head when Marcus had fallen in love with an Italian fashion designer. Paolo had wanted Marcus to come to Italy and work for him. Chloe couldn't stand in their way; besides, both she and Marcus knew that their partnership days were numbered because of their differing views.

Marcus had been fair about the price for his share of the company, but Chloe had been undercapitalized to begin with. Adding monthly payments to Marcus put a terrible strain on her cash flow. Now she needed a loan to keep on going, or she would have to close down her operation.

Chloe took a deep breath and gave Belinda a game smile. Her friends all knew her company had been on the edge for months. Every last one of them had been supportive. But this was Belinda's night. Chloe didn't want to spoil the mood of the evening. "I'm going to talk to my suppliers again. I've been a good customer in the past, and I might get them to carry me a while longer…"

Belinda grabbed her purse, which had been slung over the back of her chair, and began rummaging around for her checkbook. "Let me pay you for the shoes. There's not a reason on earth why you should give me anything so expensive. The shoes are worth a jillion times what anyone else brought."

"What?" Ariel said. "Are you disparaging that wonderful joke book I gave you on how to deal with your future mother-in-law?"

"Or the leopard silk jock strap I got for Charles?" Wendy said.

Belinda gave them a dirty look. "No, of course not. Everything was lovely. But we all know those shoes are in a different class altogether." She took the cap off her pen and flipped open her checkbook. "I know darn well they must have cost you a bundle, Chloe."

"Put away your checkbook," she said. "They're my gift to you."

"No way. At least let me pay for the actual cost of the materials. Your design is the main gift anyway. It's certainly what I'll treasure the most."

"Absolutely not," Chloe insisted. "When the day comes I can't make a pair of wedding shoes for one of my best friends, then I'm out of the business."

"Well," Angela said, "as an accountant, not to mention one of your closest and dearest friends—"

"Hear, hear," Ariel said, interrupting.

"You must let me help you with your current financial problem," Angela went on.

Ariel interrupted again. "Angela, if you're such a

hotshot financial whiz, how come you're always broke?"

"Because she's a clotheshorse," Belinda deadpanned.

Everyone howled.

"Well," Angela said, sitting up straight and obviously trying to act as dignified as possible, "I'll have you know that I'm quite solvent thanks to my recent tax refund. And even if I do spend a tad too much on clothes—" she looked around the room, daring anyone to interrupt her again "—I do know a thing or two about finance."

Angela turned to Chloe and continued, "I know you do a terrific business. Why, you can hardly read an important fashion magazine without seeing some mention of one socialite or another wearing your shoes. Maybe the problem is that you aren't presenting your business in the best light when you speak with bankers. I think I could help you with that."

Sharon spoke up. "And I'm sure we could sell a ton of your shoes at the store. We get customers who want something really upscale, like for a wedding or bar mitzvah. I'll be glad to put you in touch with our buyer."

"Thanks, both of you," Chloe said. She turned to Sharon. "I appreciate the offer, I really do, but my guess is your buyer wouldn't want to deal with me unless I delivered in quantity. And you all know how I feel about mass production. I want to be an artist who works with satin and silk and fine leathers."

"Better to be in the shoe business than not in the shoe business," Belinda said drolly.

"You're probably right," Chloe agreed. "But it may be too late to make that kind of decision. There wouldn't be time for me to get the necessary contracts to start mass production, even if I wanted to."

"There must we something we can do," Belinda said.

Chloe nodded. "There is. Let's stop talking about my problems. This is your last night with the group. I, for one, don't want to end it with a discussion about my business woes."

"Chloe's right," Ariel said. "Girlfriends, I say let's crack open one more bottle of bubbly, at my expense, and cry for our dear departed sister who is about to go off to a life of married bliss in London. Why she has decided to make one man happy when she could stay right here in good old New York and make so many men miserable is beyond me. But it's her life."

Belinda blushed. "I didn't make all that many miserable."

"Oh yeah," Angela said. "What about that awful lawyer you dated, you know, the one from Pam's firm…Grayson's friend?"

"You mean the one who spent all his time quoting baseball stats?" Belinda said.

Ariel poked her tongue in her cheek, "I thought it was ice hockey."

"No, no," Sharon said. "I had the ice hockey player. The one who had a bridge where his front teeth used to be."

Wendy giggled. Ariel rolled her eyes. Belinda smirked. "And you guys wonder why I would leave this group to marry a sensitive, intelligent man…"

"Who speaks English better than we do," Angela said, finishing the sentence for her.

Belinda grinned. "Actually, Angela, I'll bet Charles does a lot of things better than you do."

Everyone hooted. Chloe sighed with relief. At least

the others were off the subject of her now—not that she didn't appreciate that her friends cared, really cared, but this was Belinda's last meeting.

Soon the waiter arrived with Ariel's final bottle of champagne. Everyone had another glass except Chloe and Angela. During the ceremonial opening of the bubbly, Angela whispered to her that they should get together for coffee after the meeting had broken up. Chloe appreciated the offer. Angela could trade dating war stories with the best of them, but she was a sharp accountant. Any financial advice Angela might offer, Chloe wanted to hear. God knew, she didn't know where else to turn.

CHLOE ABSENTLY STIRRED cocoa while Angela finished perusing her account books. They had shared a cab and arrived back at Chloe's loft an hour earlier. As soon as she stepped out of the freight elevator, Angela had taken off her jacket and rolled up her sleeves. She sat down at the long narrow table where Donatella Morro, the wife of Carlo Morro, Chloe's cobbler, laid out the various trims when Chloe was trying to decide whether to use beads or rhinestones or feathers or buckles or bows to embellish a given pair of shoes. Carlo and Donatella were very dependable, an older couple who had been with Chloe from the day she and Marcus had started the business.

Chloe smiled to herself as she recalled Angela's comment when they'd stepped into the huge loft with its high ceilings and brick walls. "You know, Chloe, no matter how many times I visit you, I can't get over that it looks like Aladdin's cave in here."

Angela was right. The main portion of the loft was reserved for her business. The brick walls were lined with shelves holding fine leathers and skins of every possible hue, all separated by color. Creamy yellow satins and pale leathers spilled out of a shelf next to red brocades, red silks and red kid. There were brocades, satins, suedes, snakeskins, ostrich and even faux crocodile. The rainbow of colors and textures blended into a visual feast, like the biggest box of Crayolas Chloe had ever owned. Best of all, the loft always smelled of fine leathers.

"Are you sure you don't want something to drink, Angela? You've been at it for over an hour now."

Angela looked up, shaking her head. "Nope. I have a very pleasant buzz and I don't want it to disappear quite yet."

Chloe shrugged, then poured the cocoa into a mug and joined Angela at the table. Her friend gave her a determined smile as she slid the books aside.

"You know, the situation isn't all bad," Angela told her. "Just looking around I can see that you've got a ton of money in inventory. And your accounts receivable are in good shape. The real problem, as you said, is that you're overextended."

Chloe took a sip of cocoa, then pointed to a table where finished shoes were waiting for Donatella to pack and send off. "Don't I know it. Filling that order will bring in four thousand dollars, and that client always pays on time. But considering my ongoing heavy expenses, I don't have anything to fall back on when things are tight. Like now."

"You're sure you can't get a loan from your parents?"

Chloe shook her head. "They gave me a chunk of their savings to get started in the first place and with Daddy's recent heart attack, he's been talking about early retirement. In fact, I think they'd have already moved away from New York if it wasn't for me being here. He's sixty-two and, because of his health, needs to slow down. In fact, Mother's been worried sick that he pushes himself too hard."

"She's quite a bit younger than your father, isn't she?"

"Twelve years. And she insists she has no desire to be a young widow. Her latest campaign is to convince Daddy to take a short cruise with the few thousand dollars he'll get from his brother's estate."

"I understand," Angela said. She bit her lip as she gazed around the cavernous loft, the wheels obviously turning. "It's too bad you don't own this place. It would be easy to get a second mortgage on it. Then you'd have your capital infusion."

"How well I know. In fact, I was thinking about trying to buy this place with any money I might get when I sell my interest in the Cowboy Club. Mrs. Russo, my landlady, has been hinting that she wanted to unload it. She said she'd offer me a good price since it would save her dealing with real estate brokers. Of course, that was before my most recent call from my banker."

Angela blinked. "Could you run that one by me again?"

"I said, Mrs. Russo hinted that—"

"No, not that. The part about the Cowboy Club. What, pray tell, is it?"

"A bar and restaurant, at least that's the way the lawyer described it. When my uncle Cody died, he left my father ten thousand in cash, and I inherited his interest in the Cowboy Club."

"Well, kiddo, why didn't you say so? A bank will give you a loan against an ownership interest in a business, assuming the business is worth something. Where, exactly, is this club?"

"Out West, in Colorado. Some little town called Red Bluff or Red Rock, something like that."

Angela rolled her eyes. "Good God. Then it has *real* cowboys."

"I guess. You know me, I've never been west of Pittsburgh. Everything I know about the place I've heard from my father, and he doesn't know much. His older half brother went to Colorado when Daddy was just a boy. They never saw each other again and they hadn't been close as kids. But Mother kept in touch with him, writing a couple of times a year. And apparently blood was thicker than water, because Cody remembered us in his will, even though the man never laid eyes on me."

"When did all this happen?"

"I got the letter from the lawyer a week ago." Chloe went over to a file cabinet, rummaged around for a second, then pulled out a letter, scanning it as she returned to the table. "Someone by the name of Dax Charboneau holds the other half interest in the place. At least that's what the lawyer says." She handed the letter to Angela.

"Well, I say let's contact Mr. Charboneau and see if he wants to buy you out. He might be the answer to a maiden's prayers."

Chloe made a face. "Not this maiden, I'm afraid. I already called the man. It took me two days to get through to him. And you know what he said when I explained who I was? 'Little lady, this isn't New York City and I don't do business over the phone. We have a code in the West. We always deal *mano a mano*, face-to-face.'"

Angela rolled her eyes. *"Code of the West.* Is this guy for real?"

"Well, who knows. That's what he said." Chloe crossed her heart. "Honest."

"Dear God." Angela put her hand over her eyes and seemed to be concentrating. After a long silence, she looked up at Chloe and said, "Well, my dear, if Mahomet won't come to the mountain, the mountain will just have to go to Mahomet."

"Meaning?"

"That you are going to have to go to Red Rock."

"Yeah. Well, I can do the face-to-face part of it, I suppose. But considering my plumbing, how am I going to manage the *mano a mano* part?"

Angela grinned. "I have no idea. But kiddo, I'm betting on you."

2

DAX CHARBONEAU picked up the cards Wiley had dealt. An eight and the fourth queen. Showing no expression whatsoever, he watched Wiley throw in a five-dollar chip. Heath and Ford both folded. Dax raised Wiley ten. Wiley bumped Dax ten more—the final raise allowed by table rules. Dax saw the bet.

For over a year now a group of a half-dozen or so had gotten together in the back room of the Cowboy Club on Thursday evenings. Cody James and Dax had originally floated the idea of a weekly poker night. At thirty-four, Dax was the youngest, and Cody, in his late seventies, had been the oldest. Ford Lewis was in his mid-fifties, though he seemed older; Wiley was coming up on forty. Heath was only three years older than Dax. All were currently single.

"What you got, partner?" Dax said.

Wiley Cooper, who ran the newspaper, grinned from ear to ear. "Full house, jacks over sevens."

"Good hand, my friend, but not quite good enough." Without changing his expression, Dax laid his cards faceup on the table. "Four ladies. I believe that beats your full house."

Wiley groaned. "Dammit, Dax. That's three weeks in a row you've cleaned me out. At this rate you'll be owning the *Red Rock Recorder* by the end of the year."

"No chance, Wiley. A newspaperman I'm not."

"Well, God knows there isn't much around here

you don't have a piece of." Ford Lewis, who was the town's only practicing lawyer as well as the mayor, took a swig of beer as he leaned back in his chair.

Heath Barnett, a local rancher, got up from the table, stretched and turned to Dax. "Fine by me if we quit now. To tell you the truth, I sort of want to hear what happened after you talked to Cody's niece, Dax. Is she going to come out here or not?"

He shrugged. "Hard to say. I told her I wasn't about to deal with her over the phone, and I sure as hell wasn't going to go to New York City, either."

Ford, easily the oldest man in the room, shivered. "Hell, no. If she wants to talk turkey, I'd make her come to Red Rock, too. No way a person sells an interest in a place like the Cowboy Club without sitting down face-to-face. Cody himself would've demanded that, even if she is his kin. But what can you expect? An easterner and a woman, to boot."

"Well," Dax said, "for the time being we're going to have to wait and see. Lord knows, I'm in no hurry to buy her out…not with my cash reserves already committed. Hell, I can't even invest in Julia's latest scheme."

"Do you think she's really going to try to make a theme park out of that old movie set?" Heath asked.

"At Cody's wake she made it clear that she's determined to do something with the property. It would make a fine ghost town. Even Clay admitted it. Though to tell you the truth, I thought he'd choke on the words, even if he is her grandson."

"Just goes to show you what love'll do to a man," Wiley said. "Clay hasn't been the same since he got engaged to Erica."

"You can say that again. She must've addled his brains. For the life of me, I still don't understand why a good-looking guy like Clay, who could have his pick of women, would decide to settle down." Dax finished his beer and looked around. The other men were smiling at him, as if they were in on a joke he'd missed. He started to ask what he had said that was so amusing, but then decided to let it drop. "What say we ask Wanda to bring us another round? And maybe a plate of sandwiches?"

The men agreed it was too early to go home. Not that they were all that addicted to poker; the games were a chance to kick back and relax. Because of this, the sheriff looked the other way. And in truth, more than one business deal had been hammered out during a friendly game.

Dax was the only one who took the gambling halfway seriously, and that was more out of habit than anything else. But there was a time back in New Orleans when he'd lived by his wits and his poker winnings. In fact, the reason he'd come to Red Rock was that he'd won a piece of land just outside of town in a poker game. He'd owned the property nearly a year before coming to Colorado, set on selling the land and moving on. But a strange thing had happened—Dax had fallen in love with the town. It was the last thing he'd expected. An orphan who'd learned young that to get ahead he had to take chances, Dax had trusted no one, put down no roots.

He'd gotten along fine without a family or close friends. Because of his dark good looks, women had never been a problem. But he'd never really understood what all the shouting was about regarding a home and family or settling down. He had never felt the need for anything more than a real good time. Yet he realized that, deep down, a part of him must have yearned for something…unexplainable…because from his first glimpse of Red Rock, he'd wanted to stay there. It was strange, but he felt as if he belonged.

That had been nearly six years earlier. As it turned out, the piece of land he had won caught the eye of a man from Durango who wanted to put a motel on the property. Initial surveys had discovered that there was a natural spring on the land. Dax realized that could be turned to an advantage, so he offered to put up the land as his part of the venture and the man from Durango had become his partner. They built the motel/spa, capitalizing on the health benefits of the natural spring.

Two years later, they sold out. Dax took his profits and plowed the money into the Cowboy Club, which was turning out to be the best investment he'd ever made. And it was all possible because he'd been willing to take risks. Which was one of the reasons people still thought of him as a gambler—that and the fact that he always wore black.

Wanda brought in a serving plate piled high with sandwiches. Dax grabbed one. "So, what do you know about this niece of Cody's, Ford?" he asked. "He ever mention her?"

Ford picked up a sandwich. He took a bite, chewed and swallowed before he answered Dax's question.

"Well, Cody said she was in the shoe business."

"Like a cobbler...or like a shoe salesman?" Heath said.

Ford shook his head. "Neither. She designs shoes for rich women. You know, socialites like the jet-setters in Aspen, and movie stars. Cody said she even designed shoes for Princess Di before she died."

"You're kidding."

"Nope."

Dax felt his interest perk up. "How come Cody knew so much about her? I mean, his brother never came to visit or anything."

"From what Cody told me," Ford explained, "he was a lot older than his brother, who was still living at home when Cody came out here. But even though the two were not at all close, Cody's sister-in-law wrote to him a few times a year, sending pictures of his niece, keeping in touch. Cody appreciated it, and besides, the girl was his only blood relative, aside from his brother, so I guess he wanted to leave her something."

"Yeah, and a half interest in the Cowboy Club is no small thing," Wiley said.

"True," Ford agreed. "But when you consider everything Cody had, the vacant land, the commercial buildings and all the rest, he didn't give much to his family. The community church was the real winner."

"You got that right," Heath said. "From what I hear, you could've knocked Pastor Cole over with a feather when she heard the news. So far as anyone knows, Cody never set foot in a church in his life."

Dax laughed. "Maybe the old boy was hedging his bets. That would be just like him. Lordy, I miss him." He took a swig of beer. "But he sure as sin left me something to be grateful for."

"What's that?" Heath said.

"I'd rather have to deal with one little lady from New York City than Pastor Cole."

Everyone laughed.

"*Oooeee*, you got that right," Ford said. "No way do I want to tangle with Jamie. Lord knows—pardon the expression—the good pastor is as hard-driving as all get out when it comes to stretching a dollar." Ford tugged at his collar. "Makes me nervous just to think of the woman."

"Yeah," Wiley agreed, "but you can't deny, she's got the best pair of legs in town."

The other men hooted.

"Not that Wiley is hard up or anything," Dax said with a grin, "but when he told me he was going to start attending church regular-like, I figured there was more behind it than a desire to save his soul."

Wiley harrumphed. "Don't be so high and mighty, Dax. The day might come yet when you fall for a woman and decide to settle down. God knows, enough of them have tried to snag you."

"I'll second that," Ford said. "You've gone out with every eligible filly between here and Durango."

"Don't leave out Aspen, boys," Wiley said. "Day comes ol' Dax takes a fall, there'll be a headline in the *Recorder*."

Everyone laughed.

"Just trying to do my part to keep the fairer sex smiling," Dax said. "Besides, why make one woman miserable when I can make so many happy?"

Heath scratched his ear. "You know, Dax, you've had a real good run of luck since you hit Red Rock. You made a pile of dough, you have to beat the ladies off with a stick, but could be you're due for a come-uppance."

Dax cocked an eyebrow. "And why would you say that, Heath?"

"This niece of Cody's, the one from New York City. Seems to me she's in the catbird seat." Heath gave a lazy smile and looked at each man in turn. "Correct me if I'm wrong, but she owns half your club. She's your partner. And you don't have the cash available to buy her out. Have I got that right?"

Dax nodded. "So…"

"So, she's a businesswoman. Probably one of them high-powered ones with the pinstripe suits and fat shoulder pads who's used to wheeling and dealing with the big boys."

Ford rubbed his chin. "I think I see where you're going, Heath."

"Me too," Wiley said with a devilish grin.

Dax was still in the dark. "I've dealt with sharp businessmen before. You all know that. What do I have to be afraid of?"

Heath took a swig of beer, obviously enjoying that, for once, he had Dax hanging on his every word. "What're you going to do if the little lady from New York City decides that she wants to run the Cowboy Club as your partner?"

Dax opened his mouth to speak but no words came out. Of course, Heath was just putting him on. He had to be. No New Yorker would give up a prosperous business to come to a little town out West…. Well, Cody had. But that was different. He was a man.

Dax could feel his heart pound as he leaned back in his chair. Nope. He wouldn't let Heath's words rattle him. Hell, he had no reason to think Miss Chloe James would even come out here for a look-see. And if she did, so what? How much trouble could one little lady from New York City be?

CHLOE TAPPED her foot impatiently as she waited for the line to move at the car-rental counter. She was dead tired, exhausted from last-minute packing, last-minute instructions to Carlo and Donatella, last-minute advice from Angela and a last-minute prayer that she was doing the right thing.

God knew, Angela had done her best to make it easy for her. Before she'd left that night, they'd outlined a plan. By borrowing a few thousand dollars from Angela, Chloe was able to keep her business running and still travel to Red Rock. Fortunately, her design work was up-to-date and, for the next few orders at least, all that remained was for Carlo and Donatella to fabricate the shoes.

Donatella could take any incoming orders, faxing information to Chloe once she was in Red Rock. And Chloe could always fax designs back, or call her clients to talk over special needs and discuss options. Since most of her clients were international, she did much of her work over the phone anyway. She just hoped there'd be no problem finding a fax machine out West. Like a lot of New Yorkers, she wasn't certain how reliable the technology was in the little backwaters beyond the big-city lights.

Chloe moved up one space as the woman at the head of the line finally made it to the counter. Chloe looked her over. Even though the woman was renting a car, she was dressed like a local—at least, she wasn't a stranger to this part of the country. Judging by the jeans, western shirt with the sleeves rolled up and the hat, she either worked on a ranch or lived on one.

Automatically, Chloe checked out the woman's shoes. Boots. Brown cowgirl boots. Heavy and masculine. Ugly. When the woman leaned over the counter to show her driver's license, Chloe noticed how the heels were run down. Yes. This was no dude headed for a dude ranch. This woman was the real McCoy.

Glancing down at her own shoes, Chloe knew she was overdressed for Colorado. Like most business-women, she had a wardrobe of conservative, beautifully cut suits.

Chloe had grown up wearing and appreciating lovely clothes. Her mother made nearly all her outfits, which was a good thing because with her business the way it was, she couldn't afford much in the way of clothes, designer or bargain-basement. Besides, she liked knowing that her mother's hands had fabricated the things she wore. It made Chloe feel even closer to her.

For the plane trip, she'd chosen a medium-weight navy suit. Her blouse was a red silk shell and her shoes were made with the softest scarlet kid available. They had three-and-one-half-inch heels and a thin ankle strap. They were sexy but not blatantly so, and very, very chic.

From the time she was a small girl, Chloe had shared her mother's love of fashion. Martine Coquet had come to the United States as a student, eventually getting a job with a top New York designer. Over the years, she became a valued assistant and head of all the seamstresses.

Martine had met Chloe's father three years after coming to the States. It was one of her dad's favorite stories, told at the breakfast table every March 17— Saint Patrick's Day—without fail. Martine and a friend had gone to an Irish pub to celebrate. Dennis James had spotted her in the crowd. The way he told it, he'd taken one look at the vivacious French-woman and had been hooked.

At the time, Chloe's dad had owned a shoe repair shop in Queens and had dreams of opening a whole chain of shops. He'd learned the trade from his own father and liked the work, unlike his older brother, Cody.

Tapping her foot again, Chloe wondered if this trip would be the solution to her problems or a colossal waste of time. Sure, Angela had made a convincing argument—go to Red Rock and check out the Cowboy Club. Talk to bankers, fax Angela the profit-and-loss statement and see what the place was worth. In the best-case scenario, she'd get Dax Charboneau to buy her out. If that didn't work, she'd try to get a loan on the place so she'd have the capital to run her business until she could sell her interest in the club. In and out of town in a New York minute. *If* things went according to plan.

But now doubt was setting in. What if Dax Charboneau gave her a low-ball offer? Worse, what if he refused to deal with her? Heaven knew, he had certainly given her the short shrift over the phone, refusing to so much as talk about business. And she'd been in such a hurry to leave New York that neither she nor Angela had called to see if he'd even be in Red Rock!

As she thought about it, Chloe wondered if maybe she was going off half-cocked. Sure, from a financial standpoint, time was of the essence. But what did she know about the situation in Red Rock? Nothing, really.

She'd had one letter from the lawyer, Ford Lewis. The formal, almost archaic, way in which he'd phrased things made her think he must be a contemporary of Cody's, which would put him at least in his sixties. She assumed that Dax Charboneau was about that age, as well. He and Cody had probably been partners for years and years. That might spell trouble. From experience, she'd learned that older men sometimes had a problem with women in business.

When she'd first started her company, some of the older male sales reps had not been sure how to deal with her. Some wanted to flirt, others were patronizing. Marcus had offered to run interference, but Chloe knew that was not a solution, not in the long run. Instead, she had shown that she was a woman of her word, a serious businesswoman who could be taken seriously. Fortunately, she hadn't encountered situations like that for years now. But with her luck, Dax Charboneau might be a throwback, a real chauvinist. After all, he had called her "little lady," and he'd refused to do business over the phone. True, his voice hadn't sounded old, but that didn't necessarily mean anything.

Sighing, she realized that if he proved to be as bad as she feared, she'd simply have to deal with it. Be pleasant but firm. Very firm. After all, she was a New Yorker, born and bred. She wouldn't be worth her salt if she couldn't deal with one aging dandy from the back of beyond.

Assuming, of course, she ever got to Red Rock. The woman ahead of her seemed to be taking forever. Chloe was beginning to lose patience. Checking her watch, she wondered if she'd be able to make the drive to Red Rock by sunset. She'd taken an early flight to Denver. It wasn't quite noon, though she'd been up for so long she felt ready for an early dinner and bed instead of lunch and the prospect of a long drive.

"I can help the next in line," came the voice from behind the counter.

Chloe looked up with a start, realizing the young man with the hayseed haircut was speaking to her.

She picked up her bags and stepped to where he waited. "Hi," she said, smiling. No sense acting like a pushy New Yorker, she thought as she handed the man her driver's license and credit card. Living and working at a breakneck pace might play well in the Big Apple, but she was aware that people out West were a different breed entirely. She didn't want to offend anyone. That wouldn't be kind. Nor would it serve her purpose if people found her a pain to deal with. She'd simply have to try to act more like the locals. Fit in.

It seemed like forever, but finally the man handed her the finished paperwork, showed her where to sign and told her where to find the car. "Keys'll be in the ignition, ma'am. Have a good trip."

Chloe thanked him, picked up her bags and headed out the door. She took a deep breath of the fresh, springlike air. Off to the west, she could see the mountains. It seemed strange to be in an airport and actually be able to see the Rockies. This was a different world, all right. Sighing, she hurried along, telling herself that she had to adjust her thinking. Play this thing smart. If she could manage to do that, she was almost certain to wind up a winner.

IT WAS NEARLY ten o'clock by the time Chloe pulled up in front of the Cowboy Club. She parked, set the hand brake, turned off the lights and looked at herself in the rearview mirror. No doubt about it, she looked like *The Wreck of the Hesperus*. Felt like a sinking ship, too. She was exhausted. Almost too exhausted to care that the only motel she'd spotted on the way into town—a real nice one that boasted a spa—had the No Vacancy sign lit.

The last two hours of the trip had been hell. Studying her atlas back in New York, she and Angela had concluded that the drive from Denver wouldn't be bad, which was a good thing since there didn't seem to be a commercial airport close to Red Rock. After checking the distance, Angela had pronounced that Chloe ought to arrive by dinnertime—which made sense since Angela herself had driven all the way to Washington, D.C., in just under five hours only a couple of months earlier.

Angela had been wrong.

To be sure, Chloe wasn't used to driving in the mountains. But the roads were good and the scenery was gorgeous. She had never seen anything like it in her life. If she'd had the time, she'd have pulled over every few miles and gotten out to stare. But time, and money, were of the essence. She'd stopped for gas twice, and picked up a sandwich to eat in the car.

The real problem had been when she'd taken that shortcut. The main road into Red Rock made a huge loop to the west before angling back, toward the town. From the looks of the map, the shortcut would save about sixty or seventy miles. That had seemed like a great idea. Unfortunately, the two-lane, well-paved road turned into a not-so-well-paved road, and then a narrow gravel path with potholes the size of the skating rink at Rockefeller Center. She could only make about fifteen miles an hour, and at that the road was so bumpy she thought her teeth would jar loose.

The final straw had been the flat tire. There was no traffic, so she didn't have to worry about pulling over to the edge of the road. The downside, of course, was that no traffic meant no help.

Knowing she couldn't hide from the problem, Chloe had gotten out of the car and inspected the damage. No doubt about it, the tire was as flat as her bank account. God knew, she'd never changed a tire in her life, but she'd seen it done a thousand times on TV, and the basic theory didn't seem like a big deal. Half an hour later, she decided that a flat tire in the middle of nowhere, when it was getting darker by the minute, was a very big deal indeed.

She hadn't wanted to scuff her heels on the gravel road so, before she got started, she'd slipped them off. Her panty hose had torn and snagged before she made it back to the trunk, but what was a seven-fifty pair of nylons compared to handmade shoes?

Naturally she had to take every bit of luggage— and there were four pieces, mostly filled with shoes—out of the trunk so she could get to the spare, tool kit and jack. Chloe set the bags on the side of the road, set the jack in place and began pumping. Just as she was starting to make real progress, the jack suddenly slipped on some loose gravel, nicking her shin.

Chloe yelped, though more out of fear than real pain. Fortunately, the cut wasn't deep, but warm sticky blood began streaming down her leg anyway. She hobbled to the driver's-side door, reached in and got her purse, finding an old but clean piece of tissue. She plastered it to the wound to stem the bleeding, then, after a minute's rest, went back to work on the tire.

Deciding that maybe she should get the lug nuts loose before trying to jack up the car again, she started on them. The first three came off like a charm. She was about certain she had the project under control when the fourth lug nut proved to be stubborn. Determined to get the damn thing off if it was the last thing she did, Chloe really put her back into it. Unfortunately, as she gave it her last big push, she slipped and fell backward, ripping the shoulder of her jacket and extending the slit in her skirt to halfway up her thigh.

With tears of anger and frustration welling, she lay flat on her back, staring up at the nearly full moon that was rising in the evening sky, when she heard a vehicle coming down the road. Knowing she couldn't just lie there in the gravel like some hit-and-run victim, she took a deep breath, gritted her teeth and got to her feet, brushing herself off as a pickup truck rolled to a stop ten feet back from her rental car.

The driver left the engine running and the lights on as he got out of the cab of the truck. He was a cowboy, with jeans and boots and a hat to prove it, and after introducing himself as a local rancher named Heath Barnett, he offered to help. Chloe was so relieved she could have kissed him.

Heath, who appeared to be in his late thirties, took a long languorous look at her, noting the torn clothes and her bloody leg, then he glanced at the car. Scratching his cheek, he said, "Did you have that jack under there, ma'am?"

"Yes, I did," Chloe said sheepishly. "For a while, at least. It kind of flipped out."

"I expect it did. You're darned lucky it didn't take off your leg. I know a fella that got his jaw broke doing this very thing."

Chloe blanched.

"Don't worry, I'll be glad to take care of it," he said, starting to work on the fourth lug nut. "But it's a real good thing I happened by. Not too many folks use this road."

She looked around at the growing darkness, rubbing her arms to warm herself, though it wasn't truly cold. "So I've gathered. But it looked like a shortcut on the map."

He nodded. "Yep. I kinda figured it was something like that. You aren't the first that's been deceived by that little paved stretch off the highway."

Heath Barnett had gotten the final lug nut off and now had the car jacked up. He pulled off the tire and lifted the spare into place.

"Don't reckon it's any of my business," he said, "but you wouldn't be from New York by any chance, would you?"

She chuckled. "I didn't think my accent was that strong. You ought to hear my father's."

"Wasn't just that, ma'am. But this road only goes to Red Rock. We don't get many tourists, at least, not from back East. So I'm thinking you must be Cody James's niece."

Chloe's eyebrows rose. "I am. But what made you think I might be coming? I didn't know, myself, until yesterday."

Heath Barnett laughed. "There's been talk," he said, finger-tightening the lug nuts into place. "Besides, it makes sense, considerin' you now own part of the Cowboy Club and all. Never quite expected to run into you this way, though."

"It was entirely unplanned, Mr. Barnett, I assure you."

He turned back to her and grinned. "I reckon so."

Heath lowered the car to the ground, tightened the lug nuts and put the jack and tools away, then reloaded the trunk for her.

"I expect that'll get you to Red Rock. But I'd get that tire fixed proper right away, if I was you. See Billy Wicks at the Conoco. He does good work at a reasonable price. Tell him Heath sent you."

"Mr. Barnett, I can't thank you enough." She went and got her purse from the seat. "I'd like to pay you."

"Oh, I can't accept money for a neighborly deed. Besides, I'd have to report it on my income tax and my accountant's already pulling his hair out."

Chloe blinked. "You're kidding, of course."

Heath laughed. "Yep, just pullin' your leg. No, you keep your money. Kind of seems like you might need to be buyin' yourself a new outfit. That one you got on looks the worse for wear."

"You're very diplomatic," she said. "The truth is, my suit's trashed."

"If you're going to be around these parts long, you might buy yourself a pair of jeans. And some boots." He glanced down at her bare feet, taking in the torn panty hose and the bloody tissue plastered to her leg. "I expect I best let you be on your way. You still have a piece to go before you hit good road. Have a good evenin' now."

Tipping his hat, he went back to his truck. Chloe hobbled to the driver's side of the car, thanking God for country boys. If she wasn't attacked by mountain lions on the last stretch of road, she just might make it to Red Rock.

Now, two hours later, Chloe looked in the rearview mirror and sighed. There was a smudge of dirt on her cheek. Her hair was decent, but her suit was a goner. The tissue was still stuck to the blood on her shin. She carefully peeled it off but it started to ooze a bit anyway. Oh, well, she thought, at least she'd managed to save her shoes.

Knowing it wouldn't get any easier, she opened the door of the car. This certainly wasn't the kind of first impression she'd have wanted to make as the new owner of a half interest in the Cowboy Club. But she needed advice on where she might go to spend the night, and the folks inside would be able to help her with that. Besides, even if she did look like hell, they couldn't exactly throw her out! At least, she hoped not.

3

DAX DOWNED his whiskey, neat, and checked his watch for the third time in as many minutes. He was in the office, sitting in the very chair Cody James had occupied forever. Cody's memorabilia was still on the walls. Dax hadn't touched a thing, though he'd been running the operation for several years now, through Cody's illnesses and this last period of semi-retirement. At the moment, he was trying to decide if he'd been set up by his friends, or if he was about to meet the real Miss Chloe James.

Heath had called over an hour and a half earlier, saying that the lady herself was on her way into town, and that he'd seen her out on the old cutoff road. Dax had asked Heath how he knew it was her, what she looked like, what her mood and demeanor were. But good ol' Heath had refused to say another word. Said he'd done the neighborly thing by warning him, and then he'd hung up.

Dax could have killed him.

For a while after the call, he'd been sure that Heath had been putting him on. After all, when he'd spoken to Cody's niece, she hadn't sounded at all enthusiastic about the notion of coming to Red Rock. To the contrary, she'd expected him to make her an offer over the phone!

Had something changed her mind? Was Miss Chloe James, big-time shoe designer lady from New

York City, actually on her way to Red Rock? Or was Heath pulling some kind of stunt? Dax could imagine the boys hiring some obnoxious gal to come to the club and make a scene, embarrass the hell out of him, all in the name of fun. Heath himself had never been much of a tease, but the bunch of them were capable of it. And with the run of luck Dax had had at poker, he knew the boys were itching for a chance to have a laugh at his expense.

Besides, ol' Heath did have a little extra incentive to play along. Dax had taken Mary Jo Evans to the big party celebrating the opening of the new bank building last month. How the hell was he supposed to know that Heath had a thing for her, and that they'd been dating? The woman hadn't said a word to him about Heath when he'd asked her out—not a single word. Nobody had made a big deal out of it, and Heath, to his credit, hadn't seemed especially upset. Dax had apologized and things between them seemed straight. Still, he figured the prospect of getting the upper hand for once had to have some appeal for Heath.

Dax picked up his whiskey and finished the last drop that was in the glass. He'd been thinking about the club the past few weeks, the things he wanted to do when—or, maybe *if*—he gained full control. Having Cody as a partner had been a blessing. Dax had learned a lot from the old boy. But now he was ready to take full responsibility, assuming he could deal with the uncertainty.

On the surface it seemed that he and the niece had every reason to cooperate. Chances were she wanted to divest herself of her half interest as badly as he wanted it. But he was highly leveraged, so strapped it wouldn't be easy unless he used his reserves, and *they* were earmarked for a deal with Heath Barnett and Morgan Prescott, a friend of Heath's who owned one of the largest spreads in the state. They planned to form a pool of money to invest in cattle futures, and were just waiting for the right moment to get in. Dax knew it was a golden opportunity. It might even set him up for life.

Just then there was a knock at the door.

"Yo," he said.

The door opened. It was the club's long-time hostess, Wanda Ramirez. Wanda was in her early fifties, plump, her big hair white and her fake eyelashes black as coal. Her usual attire was a lacy white off-the-shoulder peasant blouse and voluminous multi-colored Mexican skirt.

"There's a lady to see you out front, sugar," she said.

Wanda, never hiding that she thought he was the cutest devil she'd ever seen, had been on familiar terms with Dax from the day they'd met. "I never call anybody mister who's young enough to be my son," she'd explained. "Hope you don't mind." He didn't because the only kind of respect that mattered to him was the kind he earned and that didn't depend on labels.

"Does she have a name?"

"She says it's Chloe James," Wanda replied, arching an eyebrow.

"And?"

"Well, you'd better come see for yourself."

Dax got up from the worn old desk that had been in this office about as long as the place had had a roof. "Should I comb my hair first?" he joked as he stepped around the big desk.

"Don't reckon it's necessary in this case, sugar."

Dax smiled to himself. The boys *had* prepared a prank. Either that or Miss Chloe James was completely disreputable. When he got to the door, he stopped. "What did you do with her, Wanda? Put her at the bar?"

"No, I stuck her in a booth off the dance floor. She asked if she could wait someplace a little more private."

"Why's that?"

Wanda gave him a level look. "Like I said, Dax, you best come see for yourself."

"Let me ask you something before you go, Wanda."

She stopped, resting her hands on her ample hips.

"Are Heath and Ford and the other boys out there?"

"Most of 'em. Why?"

"Nothing, I was just curious," he said. "Look, will you tell Miss James I'll be a minute? I want to grab my files."

Wanda left and Dax went to the file cabinet. Of course, he wasn't really going to talk serious business with whoever was out there, but he wanted to make it look as if he'd swallowed their bait. He'd act coolly professional. Not bat an eye, regardless how she looked or what she did.

He fooled around for a few minutes, taking his time with the files, figuring it'd be a good thing to let her cool her heels. The more exaggerated her behavior, and the more calm and collected he was, the better. Finally, he smoothed the collar of his black shirt, centered his silver belt buckle, picked up his files and opened the door. He walked along the short hall and out the door that accessed the club.

On nights when they didn't have live music and

dancing, and the dinner crowd wasn't especially big, they'd close off the rear dining area next to the dance floor and seat everyone in the front dining room or at the bar, which ran along one wall in the front half of the building. Dax stopped to appraise the scene. He saw his friends at the rear of the bar, nearest the dance floor. Sliding his eyes over, he spotted the woman they were discreetly watching.

She was pacing at the corner of the dance floor, her purse on the table at the nearest booth, her arms folded over her chest.

Dax's mouth sagged open. She was stunningly beautiful—he noticed that immediately—but she looked as though she'd run into trouble. Or a buzz saw. First, her jacket was torn at the sleeve and there was a big smudge of something on her cheek, grease, maybe. As she turned sharply with the flair of a fashion model with an attitude, Dax noticed the kick pleat in her skirt was ripped clear to the top of her thigh, revealing the sexiest leg he'd seen in an age. Best of all, perhaps, were her ankles, so slim the finest racehorse would be envious, especially in light of the red ankle straps on the very sexy, and very high, heels on her feet. He could only stare.

Making another sharp turn, she caught sight of him and stopped dead in her tracks. Was there fury in her eyes, or impatience? he wondered. Could this possibly be the real Chloe James?

Dax glanced over at the boys, all of whom were eagerly watching. It was a setup, he was sure. Even so, he could hardly take his eyes off the woman. She cocked her head as if to say, "Well, are you Dax Charboneau? And if so, why are you just standing there?"

Gathering himself, Dax made his way to the dance

floor, taking in the pleasing lines of her body. She was of just average height but very slender, which made her seem a little taller. And she looked to be in her late twenties. Whatever the hell was going on, he was liking what he saw.

The woman moved toward him, her expression no-nonsense. "Mr. Charboneau?"

"Ms. James?"

As she stepped forward to shake hands with him, her heel caught on the edge of the dance floor and she came flying at him like a missile. Dax dropped the files barely in time to catch her. She lay in his arms, staring up at him. Dax heard someone gasp. He was aware that the files had landed with a splat. But he ignored everything and just kept gazing into the biggest emerald eyes he'd ever seen in his life. Chloe James—or whoever she was—was gorgeous.

Dax held her by the waist and shoulder, as though they'd been slow dancing and he'd dipped her. Time seemed to stop, each beat of his heart taking a minute instead of a second. Drawing in a deep breath to pull himself together, Dax gave the lady his most wicked smile.

"Welcome to the Cowboy Club, Ms. James. I've been expecting you."

She squirmed and said, "Do you mind?"

Though a part of him sort of wanted to keep her right where she was, he helped her to stand upright. She dusted herself off.

"Dax Charboneau, I presume?" she asked.

Her cheeks were rosy with embarrassment. He liked the way she seemed sort of flustered.

"Yep. I'm Charboneau. The one and only." He bowed. "At your service, though in fairness I ought to tell you we only give free dance lessons on Tuesday nights."

Her eyes narrowed and she looked as if she wanted to slug him. Dax had to bite his cheek to keep from laughing. Instead, he inclined his head toward the booth where she'd left her purse. "Please, Ms. James, sit down and make yourself at home. I'll just pick up my files before I join you."

She didn't argue. But, as she took her first step away from him, she faltered and he had to steady her again. Apparently, her right heel had broken when she caught it on the edge of the dance floor. Dax watched as she clenched her teeth, muttering something under her breath. He thought he caught the words "Dammit to hell." Then, trying to act as dignified as possible, Miss Chloe James of New York City—or whoever she was—slipped off her shoe. She wobbled the broken heel until it came off in her hand, then she turned her attention back to him.

"You know, you could get sued for that," she said. "In New York, if anyone tripped the way I did, they'd have a whole pack of lawyers on you by the next morning."

Dax chuckled. "You mean *we* could get sued, don't you?" He saw her face fall. "But don't worry. Folks out here aren't so anxious to litigate. It so happens, the most prominent attorney in town, in fact the *only* practicing attorney, is sitting at the bar right now."

She glanced over at the bar. Heath kind of waved at her. She gave a tentative wave back, then hobbled off the dance floor.

Out of the corner of his eye, he saw Heath nudge Ford with his elbow. Dax knelt down to scoop up the files, pretending he hadn't seen the byplay. He wasn't so certain now that this was a setup. And though the woman's suit was torn and her shoes were ruined, both had New York City written all over them. Hell, he didn't even think you could buy shoes like that in Colorado, even in Denver or Aspen. Not that he was an expert or anything, but he'd been around enough women with money and style to know good clothes when he saw them.

That meant she'd either blushed because she was embarrassed at showing up like this, or she'd been reacting to him. He sure as hell hoped it was the latter, because he liked those ankles, the emerald green eyes and the way that fat black curl had fallen across her forehead, almost as much as he liked her feisty streak.

Dax smiled. He hadn't liked the idea of having an unknown for a partner, or the fact that she was from New York City. But if the woman he'd just held in his arms was the real Chloe James, then good old Cody might have done him a good turn, after all.

CHLOE WATCHED as Dax Charboneau scooped up papers and put them in file folders. For some reason, the story her father retold each year on Saint Patrick's Day about meeting her mother in an Irish pub popped into Chloe's head, how her Dad had fallen in love with Martine at first sight. Chloe thought that was so romantic. Deep in her heart she'd always hoped that the same thing would happen to her—that she'd meet Mr. Right someday and they'd be as happy as her parents had been.

But why on earth was she thinking of that now? The Cowboy Club was about as far as you could get from an Irish pub. There was an enormous buffalo head hanging behind the bar, for heaven's sake! And even though Dax Charboneau was terribly good-looking, she had no reason whatever to think he was special. None. Besides which, she'd already clashed with him.

The problem was probably that she was tired and hungry. She had to get hold of herself...not to mention her tongue. Sure, she'd had to cool her heels, waiting for more than fifteen minutes for her new partner to come out of the back room to greet her. But then, Miss Manners wouldn't have exactly approved of her dropping in unannounced. Or her smart remark about suing. Not that Dax hadn't given as good as he got, but she was the guest here, and it was up to her to put her best foot forward, even if the foot had torn panty hose and no shoes.

Chloe peered over at Dax as he shuffled through loose papers, apparently trying to decide which file to put them in. He wasn't merely good-looking, the guy was drop-dead gorgeous. And he had a kind of aura that hinted at danger, though she wasn't sure why, unless it was because he was dressed all in black. She shivered, though it wasn't from cold.

Dax Charboneau reminded her of the riverboat gamblers in the old Westerns she'd watched as a kid. The expression on his face as he'd caught her in his arms—not to mention his quick remark—had been as smooth as silk. The guy was a charmer and he knew it. To think she'd assumed that he was about the same age as her uncle!

Dax finished picking up the files. He started toward the table with file folders in hand. The hostess followed. Chloe noticed her shoes—black patent pumps with spiky three-inch heels and long pointed toes—and the way the poor woman was walking. The pumps were old enough that Chloe could see the indentation of her toes on the side of the shoe. The toe box was obviously too tight. If Chloe had to guess, the poor woman's feet were killing her.

Dax plopped the files down and slid into the banquette, moving right next to her, much closer than she would have expected. Chloe noticed the tang of his cologne. It was like sage and pine and the wind. Clean and sexy. She wondered if he was married.

"I've already told Wanda here that I'd like a whiskey," he said. "What'll you have?"

She checked out his left hand, saw that he didn't wear a ring, and smiled, trying to make up for the fact that she hadn't been friendlier before. "Water's fine. But would it be possible to get something to eat, too? I'm starving. I know it's late, and if the kitchen is closed…"

"Wanda, bring the lady a menu. No," he said, interrupting himself, "on second thought, just bring her some buffalo stew. That'll be fastest."

Wanda nodded, set two glasses of water on the table, then headed for the kitchen with the order.

"Buffalo stew?" Chloe asked, scrunching up her face.

He chuckled. "You'll like it, I promise. It's the house specialty."

"You're kidding, of course."

"Nope. We offer all sorts of dishes you might not be familiar with. I'd be glad to introduce you to them." He winked. "You do want to learn as much as you can about the Cowboy Club while you're here, don't you?"

"Of course. Everything I can," she said.

"Everything?"

The way he said it—the lilt in his voice—was so sexy that it seemed to go right through her. Was this how her father felt when he first saw her mother?

And wasn't it odd that they'd met in a bar, too? The thought no sooner crossed her mind than Chloe gave herself another mental shake. She hadn't come to Red Rock for romance, and Dax Charboneau was not the man of her dreams.

What was wrong with her, anyway? She was a businesswoman, a serious professional. Yet ever since she'd come into this club, she'd been acting strangely. Why? Sure, she was hungry and tired, but that wasn't it. Chloe thought. Maybe it was Belinda. Yes, that was it. Her friend's upcoming marriage had been on her mind. While she'd worked on the design for Belinda's wedding shoes she'd wondered if the day would ever come that she'd be making her own wedding slippers. Not that she was jealous of her friend, but Belinda's shoes were the third pair she'd made for members of the Thursday Night Club.

"So," Dax said, interrupting her thoughts as he leaned back and put his arm along the top of the banquette, "I understand you ran into a spot of trouble out on the old cutoff road."

"Trouble! You can say that again. I got a flat."

"I'm not surprised. That road is a killer."

"Well, it darn near killed me. If that nice Mr. Barnett hadn't happened along, I'd still be there, trying to get that last lug nut off."

"I take it that's how you got…mussed up?"

She rolled her eyes. "No need to stand on ceremony. I know I look like I've been through a hurricane. But I never changed a tire before in my life. And I wouldn't have shown up like this except that the only motel I passed coming into town was full, and I figured someone here might be able to tell me where I might spend the night."

"What sort of accommodations do you have in mind?"

The first thought that popped into her head was that she wouldn't mind spending the night with him. That was crazy. She didn't even know the man and she'd never had a one-night stand in her life. It wasn't her style. Again, as she looked around the room, wondering why she couldn't keep her mind on business—serious business, not monkey business! "Anything with clean sheets will do," she said, finally answering his question. "It's been a long day and to tell you the truth, I'm bushed."

"Well, we only have the one motel, but I'll see what I can do." With that, he slid out of the booth and headed for the front of the club, where Wanda was standing by the door.

She watched as they conferred, wondering what the hostess could possibly do to help, unless she knew of someone who ran a bed-and-breakfast place in town, and that didn't seem likely. Chloe took a sip of water, then another. It tasted sweet and fresh. Just then, a man with a white jacket and chef's hat approached the table with a steaming bowl, which he placed before her.

"Your buffalo stew, Ms. James," he said. "My name's Ben, by the way. I run the kitchen. Welcome to the Cowboy Club, and if I can get you anything else, just let me know."

She thanked him, then leaned over to smell the stew. The fragrance was heavenly. Dax and Wanda were still talking up front. Chloe was so hungry she decided not to wait. The first bite came as a surprise. The meat was so tender, much more so than beef. And the flavor was wonderful. She tasted a rich red wine in the sauce—her French mother would approve of that. There were potatoes and mushrooms and even rock shrimp in the stew. Now that she thought about it, she was sure she'd read somewhere that buffalo was lower in cholesterol than beef, or even skinless chicken.

She was about half finished eating when Dax finally returned to the table. Wanda was right behind him.

"I'm so sorry I didn't wait," she began, "but you didn't order and to tell you the truth, I couldn't resist." She set down her fork. "This is absolutely delicious, by the way. Thanks so much for ordering it for me."

Dax managed to look sexy and smug at the same time. "We aim to please. And with that in mind, Wanda here has kindly offered to take you in for the night."

"Oh, I couldn't impose," Chloe said quickly.

"Nonsense, honey. I've got a spare room with a nice bed all made up and ready for guests. Used to be my daughter's, but she moved to Colorado Springs about twelve years ago, and the room hardly ever gets used these days. Besides, it'd be my pleasure."

Chloe looked at Dax and he nodded. "Well, then, I'd be most grateful. And I promise not to impose long. With luck, I should be able to get a room in the motel first thing tomorrow morning."

"That might not be necessary," Dax said. "Wanda pointed out that Cody's house is still vacant. He willed it to the community church, but I'm fairly certain our minister wouldn't object to your using the place while you're in town. We'll contact Jamie in the morning."

"Oh, that would be terrific."

"Good," Wanda said. "That's settled then. Now, if

you'll excuse me, I have a few things to do before I can leave. I know you must be dying to get someplace where you can change out of those clothes."

The hostess left and Dax returned to his seat, sliding in next to her again. Chloe could feel the heat of his body as she picked up her fork. Though she was still hungry, she paused self-consciously when she felt his eyes on her mouth.

Was he like that with every woman he encountered? she wondered. Or was it her? Chloe took another sip of water. It was late. Too late for her to think straight, that was for sure. But tomorrow would be a different matter. By light of day the man might not seem so attractive...and she'd undoubtedly be in a better position to judge what she was up against. Yes, tomorrow would be a different matter.

CHLOE MOVED the map of Colorado off the passenger seat so that Wanda Ramirez would have room to sit. The older woman slid in with a groan and pulled the door shut. Chloe hobbled around to the driver's side and got in, tossing her shoes and purse into the back seat. She'd have to drive barefoot unless she wanted to unpack and get out another pair of shoes, but Wanda had assured her they had only three blocks to go.

She started the car and backed out of the parking spot. "Which way?" she asked, turning to Wanda.

"Straight ahead two blocks, then turn right, on Colorado Street. I'm the second house from the corner. The white one with green shutters, on the left."

Chloe put the car in gear. "It must be nice, living so close to work."

"Sure is. Most nights I walk home. If there's a lot of tourists in town, like in the summer, one of the boys from the club comes along with me. Or in bad weather I get a ride. But it's a real nice walk in good weather." She paused a second. "At least, it is when my feet aren't killing me."

After another minute of driving, Chloe reached Colorado Street. She put on the turn signal. "Yes, I couldn't help noticing your shoes, and that they seemed to be pinching your toes." She gave Wanda a quick glance as she turned the corner, pulled up in front of the house with the green shutters and turned off the engine. "I'm in the shoe business, you know."

Wanda nodded. "That's what I heard. You design real fancy shoes, isn't that right?"

"I design *all* kinds of shoes. And I'll bet I could come up with something that would fit you better than what you've got on."

"Well, honey," Wanda said, "that wouldn't take much. Right now these tired old dogs are ready to call it a night. I swear, I can't possibly be as old as my feet feel."

Chloe laughed and got out of the car. Wanda got out as well, and joined her at the trunk.

"Do you need to take in everything? I always do," Wanda said. "My husband never could understand that, but I always figured I wouldn't have packed it in the first place unless I thought I was going to use it. And if I might need it, why on earth would I want it in the trunk of the car instead of in my room?"

"Wanda, I have a feeling we're going to get along just fine. That's my philosophy, too." With that, Chloe started taking her cases out of the car. Fortunately, the suitcases all had wheels. Wanda grabbed the first two and started up the walkway. Chloe retrieved her purse and shoes from the back seat, including the broken heel, then got the last of the luggage. By the time she made it to the front door, Wanda was already inside, the lights were on, and Wanda herself had pulled off her shoes, sat down and was massaging her foot.

"I declare, these feet would go on strike if they could."

Chloe smiled as she set everything down and closed the door. She stepped over to the dark blue easy chair with the green and blue afghan draped over it where Wanda was sitting, and picked up one of the offending shoes. "Do you mind?" she asked.

"Honey, you can take the damn things out front and run your car over them a couple of times for all I care."

Chloe chuckled at Wanda's suggestion, but she examined the shoe carefully. Judging from the places where it was worn, she had been right, the toe box was way too small. Not just too narrow, but also not deep enough for Wanda's toes. And with a heel that high, and a short vamp, the poor woman must have been in agony.

"Do you mind if I look at your foot?" Chloe asked.

"Feel free." Wanda extended her right foot and Chloe cupped it in her hand, checking out the three corns and the bunion. Then she looked over the left foot. The bunion was much smaller and her only corn was on her little toe.

"As sad a sight as you've ever seen, I'll bet," Wanda said.

Chloe shook her head. "Not at all. I may design expensive shoes for some of the world's best-dressed women, but I can guarantee you, several of them have bunions that would put yours to shame." She smiled as she put Wanda's foot down. "I could design a shoe for you that would be much more comfortable, if you'd like."

"Oh, I'd like," Wanda said. "But I don't think I could afford it. My husband died sixteen years ago, and we didn't have much set aside. I need my job at the club to make ends meet. And though Dax pays me real well, I can't afford fancy duds. I have two pair of shoes I wear at the club, these and some white ones, and a pair of old tennis shoes I use when I mow the lawn. That's it."

"It would be my pleasure to do it for free—"

"Honey, I couldn't let you."

"Why ever not? You've taken me in."

"That's different."

"Not to my way of thinking. Besides, if I'm half owner of the club, then you work for me just as much as for Dax. And it's in my interest to have my employees doing a good job. Nobody can do that when they're in pain."

Wanda sighed. "You're right about that."

"It's settled, then. I'll come up with a design before I go to bed tonight and fax it to Carlo tomorrow—he fabricates my shoes and is a genius with leather. Between the two of us, I can guarantee you, you'll wind up with a pair of shoes that won't hurt your feet."

"Honey, if you can do that, you can do anything." She paused for a minute, then said, "You weren't thinking about staying in Red Rock, were you?"

Chloe thought of Dax's questions and wondered if Wanda was concerned that she would try to assert herself at the club, maybe change things. "No. Why do you ask?"

"Because the women of this town sure could use someone like you."

"Well, thanks. But I don't think most of them

would like the kinds of shoes I tend to make. Not that I'm complaining, mind you, but I have noticed that a lot of the women in Colorado seem to wear boots. Cowgirl boots.''

"And you don't do boots?"

"Oh, of course I do. Riding boots, low boots to wear with slacks, dress boots to wear with certain outfits…''

"But not cowgirl boots?"

She shook her head. "I wouldn't know where to begin."

Wanda smiled enigmatically. "Well, you know, Chloe, that might change before you leave Red Rock.''

4

CHLOE OVERSLEPT. At least, she thought she had when she looked at her watch, which was still on New York time. When she noticed the clock on the night table, she realized she'd only had six hours of sleep. Not that she hadn't gotten to bed at a decent hour—at least by Colorado standards—but after she'd finished designing the sandals for Wanda, she'd lain awake for hours, thinking about Dax Charboneau.

Before she'd left the Cowboy Club the night before, Dax had suggested that they get to know each other better before they got down to business. Chloe wasn't sure how to take that. But Dax was her partner, and whether she sold her interest in the club to him or someone else, she needed to stay on his good side. Besides, she was only going to be in town for a few days and she could hardly get into trouble in that length of time.

That said, she didn't know how she would handle the strong attraction between them—and it had been mutual, she was sure of it. At least, the vibes had been there last night. But she couldn't dwell on that. She had to keep her mind on business. Carlo and Donatella were depending on her. And so were Angela and her customers.

Chloe put on her robe and looked over the sketch of the sandal she had designed for Wanda. The platform shoe would give the illusion of height without the painful pressure on her toes that she felt with high heels.

The sandals would be made of several different colors of leather, each thin strap one of the colors in the Mexican skirts Chloe found out Wanda favored. By using leftover strips of quality leather—strips that were too small to be used by themselves anyway—Chloe would be able to keep the cost way down. All that remained was to show the sketch to Wanda. If she liked it, Chloe could fax the design and proper measurements to Carlo before lunch.

As she opened the door to her bedroom, Chloe smelled the aroma of fresh coffee. She heard the sizzle of bacon and the voices of two women—Wanda and someone else.

Chloe cinched the belt of her robe and headed for the kitchen. Wanda was at the range, turning bacon, when Chloe came into the room. Wanda looked over her shoulder at her and said, "'Morning, honey. Meet Jamie Cole, the minister of the community church."

Chloe turned to see an absolutely gorgeous redhead put down her coffee mug and stand, offering her hand. She was less like Chloe's idea of a minister than anyone she'd ever seen in her life. Jamie had thick, waist-length copper hair that was pulled back in a French braid. She was slim as a young boy, and tall—close to six feet.

"Nice to meet you, Miss James. And welcome to Red Rock. I knew your uncle well. He was a fine man and I'm sorry you didn't have a chance to get to know him. I know it would have meant a lot to him."

Chloe was touched by the kind words. "Thanks for saying so. And please, call me Chloe."

"Fine. I'm Jamie."

Wanda turned from the stove to say, "I hope we

didn't wake you, honey. Jamie and I have been chatting away while I cook, and I plumb forgot you might want to sleep in."

"Oh, no. I've been awake for a while anyway."

The minister sat down and, after offering to help Wanda and being refused, Chloe joined Jamie at the table. A basket of blueberry muffins was there, and a big glass of orange juice. She took a sip of juice before breaking open a muffin. It was so hot that steam came out of it.

Wanda turned from the range. "Bacon is almost done. How do you like your eggs, honey?"

"Oh, heavens, you don't have to wait on me, Wanda."

"Might as well, considerin' you're my new boss." She winked. "Need to make a good impression."

Chloe laughed. "Then how about scrambled?"

"Fine."

Jamie took up the conversation. "Dax called me last night and suggested that you might want to stay in your uncle's place while you're in town. I think it's a terrific idea. We could go over after breakfast, if you want, and check out the place. It's small, only a couple of bedrooms, a tiny kitchen and bath, and a living room."

"Heavens," Chloe said. "I don't need anywhere near that. I was expecting to get a motel room."

"Then Cody's house ought to work just fine. You'd have more room, and more privacy, too. We'd just have to get the bed made and air the place out."

"That sounds wonderful. I appreciate your offer. And I'll be glad to pay your church whatever I was going to pay for a motel."

"I won't hear of it," Jamie said. "Cody was incredibly generous to leave us so much of his property. It's the least we can do."

Wanda put a plate of bacon on the table and a mug of coffee. "Eggs will be done in a minute," she said.

Chloe took a sip of coffee. It was strong and rich. "I can't tell you how much I appreciate this. Everyone here has been so kind."

"Not as kind as you've been to me...if those new shoes you talked about fit," Wanda said.

Chloe chuckled. "Oh, they'll fit, all right. There's nothing like custom shoes."

Jamie seemed puzzled, so Chloe explained. "Her feet were killing her last night. I have a company that makes custom shoes, and I offered to design a pair for Wanda that'd fit better than her old ones and still be attractive. In fact," she said, rising from the table, "let me get the design now, Wanda, and you can tell me what you think."

Chloe went to her room for the sketch. When she returned, Wanda was setting a plate of scrambled eggs on the table. Chloe sat down again. She handed over the design for the sandals before helping herself to eggs and bacon. Everything looked good.

Wanda oohed and aahed before she showed the drawing to Jamie. "These are so beautiful, Chloe. And I love the way they have so many colors in them. They'll go with everything I have."

Chloe swallowed a bite of bacon. "Good. I particularly thought they'd go with your Mexican skirts...you said that was what you usually wore to work. And with all the various colors of leather, the shoes will be festive. Best of all, the platform will give you some height without killing your poor toes."

"Well, I don't know what to say. I'm real thankful."

Jamie regarded the drawing. "These truly *are* beautiful." She looked down at her cowgirl boots. "I hate to admit it after seeing these sandals, but ninety-nine percent of the time I wear jeans and boots. A lot of the women in town do."

Chloe took another bite of blueberry muffin. "But you must wear dress shoes sometimes, don't you?"

"I put on heels for Sundays, of course. And for weddings and baby ceremonies." Jamie gave her a wry smile. "The rest of the time I tend to look like I just got off my horse."

"Do you have a horse?" Chloe asked, wide-eyed.

Jamie laughed. "Of course. I was brought up in Red Rock on a ranch."

"Well, sort of brought up," Wanda interjected. "As I recall, you were considered the town hellion. We weren't sure you'd make it there for a while." She paused to wink at Chloe. "Could have knocked me over with a feather when you wound up our minister. Damnedest case of conversion I ever did see. No offense meant, Jamie."

"And none taken." Jamie turned to Chloe. "Wanda isn't exaggerating. But there is an advantage to having a past. I get along real well with the youth. They know they can't get away with anything, because I already did it years before and I'll know what they are up to."

"I'm sure you weren't as bad as all that…"

"Oh, she was worse," Wanda said. "Fact is, Jamie here burned down the bell tower of the church when she was twelve."

Suppressing a giggle, Chloe turned to Jamie, who nodded.

"It's true. Quentin Starr and I were smoking. He was fourteen and should've known better…of course, I should have, too. But when old Miss Hodges, the church secretary, nearly caught us, I threw my cigarette into the bell tower. It landed on some papers and caught fire."

"Oh my."

"You can say that again." She laughed. "But I've made amends. And I love my work, especially the weddings. I was thrilled to death when Clay McCormick asked me to marry him and Erica."

"I didn't know they'd set the date," Wanda said.

"Oh yes. The first Saturday of next month...about three weeks from now. Julia is as pleased as punch."

Wanda turned to Chloe. "Julia Sommers is Clay's grandmother. And she was your uncle's partner in the Cowboy Club until she sold her interest to Dax. That was a few years ago now."

"I see. So, Julia and Clay are connected to the Cowboy Club, too?"

"Chloe, damn near everyone in town is connected with the club," Wanda said. "And if you hang around long enough, you'll find out why."

She didn't know what to make of that, so she concentrated on finishing her breakfast instead.

CHLOE WAS SITTING on the floor of her room, going through her suitcase full of shoes and trying to decide which ones to wear for her lunch meeting with Dax, when there was a knock on the door. It was Wanda.

"Come on in," Chloe said.

"Honey, I just wanted to tell you goodbye. I have an appointment at the beauty shop. You're in good hands with Jamie. Just be sure to lock the front door on your way out, and I'll see you at the club later on."

Chloe got up from the floor and took Wanda's hand in both of her own. "Thanks so much for taking me in last night, and for that wonderful breakfast. I don't know how to thank you."

"Honey, if those fancy sandals of yours can keep my bunion happy and my corns from complainin', that's more than enough." She gave Chloe's hand a final squeeze. "Now don't you get into trouble with Jamie."

She smiled. "I won't. In fact, why don't you send her in here? Maybe she can help me decide which shoes to wear today."

Wanda left. Chloe heard her say something to Jamie before the front door opened and then closed. Wanda was a real pistol. In fact, now that she thought about it, everyone in Red Rock seemed larger than life. Dax, Wanda, Jamie. Even that nice guy out on the cutoff road who'd rescued her.

"Hey, Chloe," she heard the minister call out from the other room. "How about I bring you another cup of coffee while you finish dressing?"

"Sounds good to me," she replied.

Chloe turned back to the task at hand. She'd brought quite a few clothes with her but they were mostly business attire. Last night at the Cowboy Club she had noticed that most of the women were dressed casually. Of course, she hadn't expected people to dress as if they were going to a New York supper club, but even the most casual things she had with her were still way too formal by Red Rock standards.

Her mother had taught her to take pride in her appearance. She was always well groomed, especially when working. After all, she was her own best representative for her shoes, and the most effective way to show them off was to be appropriately dressed.

But now, her clothes were a problem for the first time in her life. Here in Red Rock, jeans and boots seemed to be called for. Most of the women in the club the night before had been dressed like latter-day Annie Oakleys, and Chloe had seen more cowgirl boots there than in her entire life. This morning, Jamie had worn a western shirt, Levi's and boots. Only Wanda had broken the trend. She'd put on plain navy slacks that morning and a white long-sleeve blouse. Chloe knew she would stick out like a sore thumb.

She sighed just as Jamie entered the room, carrying two steaming mugs of coffee. She handed one to Chloe, who took a sip.

"I'll say one thing for Colorado," Chloe said. "You folks sure know how to make good coffee, even if it isn't latte."

Jamie laughed. "Oh, you can get fancy coffees out here, too. The Cowboy Club has espresso. But most folks here like things plain."

"So I've noticed." Chloe pointed to the black slacks of fine wool crepe that she'd laid out to wear along with a taupe jersey V-neck sweater. The outfit would look terrific for a day of antiquing in Connecticut. "To tell you the truth, Jamie, I feel like a fish out of water. I have all the wrong clothes. Just look at those pants."

The redhead reached over and felt the material. "They're beautiful. I can tell you right now that half the women in town would kill to have clothes like these."

"But I'll be overdressed."

Jamie shrugged. "You are who you are, Chloe. Go with it. There is nothing worse than trying to be something you aren't."

"You mean I shouldn't run out and buy jeans and cowgirl boots," she teased.

"Afraid not. At least, not just because you think

you have to fit in. Folks in Red Rock tend to be tolerant. And the West has always catered to strong individuals. Julia Sommers, for example."

"The woman who used to own the club with my uncle? The one who sold out to Dax?"

"That's right. Julia was from Hollywood. She came out here to make a movie. Not that she was a star or anything, but she had a substantial part in two or three films. Then she married Hap and they were as happy as a couple of clams. Of course, Julia, being Julia, always did have a dash more glamour than the rest of us, but no one thought any less of her because she liked to wear sequins and bangles."

"I suppose you're right. I shouldn't worry about it. Besides, I probably won't be around long enough for it to matter."

"Then you aren't planning on keeping your interest in the Cowboy Club?"

Chloe shook her head. "I don't know the first thing about the restaurant business, or bars or cowboys or the Wild West, for that matter. Investing in something you don't understand is usually a big mistake. Besides, I really need whatever money I can get out of the club for my own business."

"Well, you ought to have plenty of takers. The club is real popular. Sort of the heart of the town in a lot of ways."

"Good, because I don't have much time to find a buyer. I can't afford to be away from New York indefinitely, either financially or otherwise. In fact, the truth is, I was sort of hoping Dax would be interested in buying me out."

"I have no doubt he will be. I've heard him say the Cowboy Club is the crown jewel of his investments. It is very important to him."

Chloe recalled the way Dax had charmed her the

night before. Had he truly been attracted to her, or was he simply trying to take control of the situation? It had sure felt real, but there was no way to know for sure. "Oh?" she said innocently. "And why is that?"

Jamie sat down on the second twin bed, the one that didn't have clothes or a suitcase on it. "Dax grew up in New Orleans—but he loves Red Rock. And he was real close to your uncle."

"So did he buy Julia's interest in the club because he wanted to be partners with Cody?"

"I don't think so. They became good friends after Dax bought her out. I believe Dax wanted a piece of the Cowboy Club because that way he'd be in the center of action. As I said, the club is really the heart of the town."

"Yes, Wanda alluded to that, too. But why?"

Jamie sighed. "It's not so easy to explain." She pulled off her boots and sat cross-legged on the bed. Chloe noticed that the minister's socks were yellow and had pink roses on them. The whimsy made her smile. "It's a feeling, a mood, more than anything," Jamie said by way of explanation. "Back in the forties and fifties, when a lot of Westerns were filmed in these parts, the movie stars went there every night. If you go back into Cody's office, you'll see their pictures. John Wayne, Gary Cooper, Maureen O'Hara, Glenn Ford and Henry Fonda. They were out filming at the fake western town...the place Julia calls her 'ghost town,' and at night they came to the club to have dinner and rub elbows with the real cowboys." Jamie took a sip of her coffee.

"And there was a sort of romance about that, romance with a capital R, that rubbed off onto the place. It's everyone's special hangout—often as not, where they first fell in love."

Chloe thought of last night. When she'd seen Dax

picking up those files, the first notion that popped into her mind was how her parents had also met in a bar. And she hadn't been able to keep romance off her mind. But that didn't necessarily mean that the Cowboy Club itself had anything to do with it. "But isn't it the only restaurant of its size in town?" she asked logically.

"I don't think that's it. There have been other places to dine over the years. The Elk's Club is plenty big for weddings and anniversary parties. People go to the Cowboy Club because it makes them *feel* special."

Chloe recalled the way she'd responded to Dax the night before. Was that what Jamie was talking about? "Has the club ever affected you in any kind of special romantic way?" she asked.

Jamie shook her head. "Nope. But my reputation as the town hellion hasn't done me much good. And now that I'm a minister, well, lots of men would wonder if I was too pure…too good for them."

"Damned if you do, damned if you don't. Is that it?"

The minister chuckled. "In a manner of speaking. Though I don't kid around about that in my line of work."

Jamie finished the last of her coffee and excused herself to go to the bathroom. Chloe took the opportunity to put on her sweater and pants. She was standing over her suitcase, still in her stocking feet, when the redhead returned.

"As soon as you're finished, I'll help you take the luggage out to the car," Jamie offered.

"Thanks," Chloe said. "The only thing left to decide is which shoes to wear."

Jamie cast her eyes over the assortment of shoes lined up on the floor next to the bed. "That's one problem I never have," she said, picking up a brown alligator pump and sighing. "Though to tell you the truth, for shoes half as elegant as these, I could give up my frugal ways. In fact, it would be hard not to get downright greedy."

Chloe laughed. "Thanks for the compliment. But believe me, after a while, you take custom-made shoes for granted, just like anything else." She quickly narrowed the field down. "Believe it or not, deciding which shoes to wear is my biggest decision every day."

"I do believe it. With so much to choose from, it would be hard." Jamie picked up the dressiest pair of shoes Chloe had brought, silver kid heels with narrow straps that crossed over the top of her foot in an X. "I've never in my life seen anything so delicate. These are fit for a queen."

Chloe nodded as she started putting shoes into shoe socks so she could repack them. "I made a pair exactly like that for a duchess."

"Really?"

"Yes. She was going to a ball in Venice and was wearing a silver gown. The shoes were made to match, but they had to be exceptionally well balanced because the duchess wanted to dance the night away."

"And did she?"

"Who knows. I'm still making footwear for her, so I must have done something right." After putting the silver shoes away, the only two pair left out were some low boots with a flat heel in a soft black suede that zipped up to the ankle, and a pair of black kid pumps that had an open toe. The pumps weren't high, having only a two-and-a-half-inch heel. "What do you think?"

Jamie picked up the boot, running her finger over

the suede. Then she picked up the pump. "You're having lunch with Dax?"

Chloe nodded.

"Then I vote for the pump."

"Any particular reason?"

The redhead grinned. "They're a lot sexier than the boots. And, well, I couldn't help noticing your feet. Your toenails are such a pretty shade of bright pink, and with the pumps, you'll be able to see them."

Chloe arched an eyebrow. "And is that important?"

"To Dax it might be."

Chloe wasn't quite sure what to say to that, though by Jamie's sly smile she knew the minister was half kidding. Still Chloe couldn't help wondering if Dax would notice her toes. And if he did, what would it mean?

5

Dax looked in the mirror. He'd shaved real close that morning. He'd put on his newest shirt that was just back from the laundry, and his best black snake-skin boots. His hair was a little shaggy, but he didn't have time for a haircut.

Normally, he never gave two hoots about how he looked. He always wore black; he always wore boots. With his coal black hair and deep blue eyes, he'd never had a problem attracting the ladies. From the time he was fifteen they had been coming on to him. He'd dated rich women, poor women, older women and younger ones. None had ever gotten under his skin.

Until now.

When he'd walked out of his office the night before and seen Chloe James pacing by the edge of the dance floor, something had snapped inside him. Sure, she was beautiful, but he'd seen beautiful women before. So what was it?

He closed his eyes and pictured the expression on her face as she'd looked up at him after he'd caught her. She was blushing, and there was something in her eyes, a sort of challenge, maybe, that had gotten to him. He wanted to know what she was thinking. He needed to find out what was behind the smile, the laugh, and all the unsaid things that she was holding back.

Most of all, he wanted to see the look in her eye

when he made love to her for the first time. And there would be a first time—if it killed him. He wanted this woman in every sense of the word and was determined to have her.

That had happened before, of course, lots of times. More often than not, she was just as attracted to him, and it was easy. But this time it wouldn't be so easy because their relationship was rife with complications. Chloe James was half owner of the Cowboy Club, which meant she had all sorts of leverage and he had to avoid a screwup.

He needed to cut a deal with her because if he didn't, sure as shootin', someone else would. The trick would be to gain her confidence, make her like him enough that she'd want to sell to him and him alone. If they had a little romance along the way, that was all to the good. The key was to keep it light. A nice simple fling. A flirtation. Then, once the deal was done, all bets would be off.

Dax pictured Chloe with those long legs of hers wrapped around him as he made love with her. He could visualize the way her emerald eyes would darken with passion when he entered her. He wanted Chloe James as he hadn't wanted a woman in a long, long time.

He groaned. Hell! If he wasn't careful he was going to wind up like Clay McCormick—headed for the altar with a city girl. What a joke that would be. Dax still didn't understand what had happened there. He and Clay had been close, once spending a weekend together in Vegas. They'd partied with a couple of gals they met in a casino and when it was time to leave the women, they'd both said adios with no regrets. Dax figured that he and Clay were two of a kind.

Then Erica Ross had rolled into Red Rock and his

friend had folded like a poker player with a bad hand. Dax just didn't understand it, and he'd told Clay so. "Why get married? I mean, sure, Erica's great. But there are so many wonderful women around. What do you want to tie yourself down for?"

Clay had looked at him long and hard before he answered. "Because I love her, Dax. And I can't imagine life without her."

"I still don't get it, partner," he'd said, shaking his head.

Clay had gotten a real sad look in his eye. "That's because you've never belonged to a family. You don't realize what you're missing."

He had allowed that was so, and out of respect for Clay he'd let the subject drop. But later, he'd thought of their conversation again. Clay's reminder had sort of gotten to him. Dax had been on his own from day one, in a sense.

But the fact that he'd never had a family didn't really matter. After all, he was happy, wasn't he? He had friends. He made a good living. He had a home, a business and a life. And so far as marriage and a family was concerned, hell, he didn't have to be an expert on family life to know it wasn't for him.

Nope, he thought as he took a final look in the mirror, he was not a candidate for any commitment longer than a date the following weekend. Why he was even thinking along these lines, he had no idea.

CHLOE SAT on the bed she had just finished making in her uncle's house and looked around. She was alone now. Jamie had gone with her to the grocery store where she had gotten a few things to tide her over—milk, cereal, bread, eggs and some lunch meat for sandwiches. Then the minister had to go visit a sick congregant. But they had agreed to keep in touch. She was glad. Jamie Cole was one of the nicest women she'd ever met.

Chloe got up from the bed and wandered into the second bedroom that Cody had used as a home office. She sat down at the old oak rolltop desk. Tacked to the bulletin board on the wall next to the desk she saw a group of pictures of Cody with his friends. In one he was standing next to Dax. In another shot he was with Wanda and a couple that she didn't recognize.

Up in the top corner of the corkboard, she spied the last Christmas card her mother had sent, along with her annual Christmas letter. Several pictures of Chloe at various stages of her life were also tacked to the board. Chloe was touched. How was it that this man, her father's brother who had never even laid eyes on her, could have found it in his heart to be so generous to her, especially when he had so many good friends in town?

Cody had obviously cared for her. Or at least, he'd cared for the *idea* of her. That made her wonder why her uncle had never married and had a family. Perhaps he'd been generous to her because she was as close as he'd ever gotten to having a child of his own. And that was so sad, particularly since she'd never had a chance to know him. She might have been able to bring some extra measure of joy into Cody's life, to help justify and repay the gift he had given her.

Chloe sighed. When she'd gotten the letter from Ford Lewis telling her that she'd inherited a half interest in the Cowboy Club, she'd been pleased because it had been like a godsend—a way to get the cash reserves she needed. Now...well, she felt differently. Oh, she still wanted to save her business, but it was also important to her that she come to a fuller understanding of what the club had meant to her uncle. To do any less would not honor his gift.

The big unknown in the equation was Dax Charboneau. If Jamie was right, and he wanted to purchase her interest in the club, she'd have to forget that he was so deliciously sexy. She'd mixed business and pleasure once in the past, and had learned the hard way that it didn't work. She wouldn't go down that road again.

After checking her watch she decided she might as well head for the club. She wasn't due to meet Dax for another forty-five minutes, but she'd hardly seen a thing of the town the night before because it was already dark. She would drive to the club and then walk around a bit before lunch.

Grabbing her purse and key, Chloe carefully locked the front door of the tidy little house and went out to the car. Cody's home was a bit farther from the club than Wanda's house had been, but in the opposite direction, meaning she was about six or seven blocks from Wanda's place.

Chloe got in her rental car and drove to the business district of Red Rock, parking a couple of blocks away from the Cowboy Club. She got out of the car in front of a vacant brick building. Gold lettering across the window proclaimed that the place had once been a saddlery.

Chloe cupped her hands and peered in the window. The building was obviously being renovated. She liked the old brick interior walls—they gave the place character. But it surprised her that a saddlery would go out of business. With so many ranches in the area, she'd have thought that would be a booming enterprise.

She started down the sidewalk. The Cowboy Club was on the opposite side of the street, in the middle of the second block. The businesses on either side of it—a rock shop and men's western-wear store—had the same weathered frame front. It was obvious that stretch of buildings had been around for decades and was probably the oldest part of the town. And the wooden boardwalk on that side of the street really gave the businesses character.

Chloe passed the post office, the feed store and a beauty shop. She glanced in the beauty salon, wondering if that was where Wanda got her hair done. But when she didn't see her, she walked on. She came to the newspaper office, the *Recorder*, which was directly across from the Cowboy Club. She looked at the most recent edition of the paper that was put up in the window. Scanning the front page, she saw news of an expansion of the local library and an article about bald eagles having returned to the Lone Eagle Ranch.

She smiled, thinking about the articles in the *New York Times*. Most were about crime or politics. Sometimes she was so sick of both that she skipped the front page and went straight to the human-interest stories. It occurred to her then that, in a way, Red Rock was *all* human interest. The men and women who lived here knew their neighbors—not just the people in their building or those who worked on the same floor of their offices.

People here grew up together, went to school together, worked and worshiped together. It was a community. Her uncle had been a part of it. And now, at least for a while, she was a part of it, too. And all because she'd inherited his interest in the Cowboy Club.

Her eyes turned to the club, just across the street. Suddenly, she recalled what Jamie had said about the place—that it was the heart of the town. Chloe kind of liked that. She liked knowing that she had a little piece of what had made this community a place where family and neighbors meant something.

She also remembered what else Jamie had said. That the club had a magic about it, the kind of magic that made people fall in love. That was nonsense, of course. It had to be. Even if she had felt a strong attraction to Dax Charboneau, there was no reason to think it had anything to do with the Cowboy Club. After all, the guy *was* a hunk. And sexual attraction had been around for millions of years. There was nothing magical about it.

Yet the more she had talked to Jamie, the more she realized how down-to-earth the minister was— hardly the type who'd exaggerate. Now Chloe wished she'd asked a few more questions.

She again thought about the night before, when she'd first entered the club. Had she felt anything special? She didn't think so. Of course, she'd been too tired and too embarrassed about the way she looked to pay much attention to the mood of the place. And when she had made a spectacle of herself by falling into Dax's arms in front of half the town, all she'd thought of was how she could recover some semblance of dignity.

The real test would be today, and she doubted that she'd notice anything. In fact, now that she really thought about it, the reason she'd overreacted was obvious—it had been way too long since she'd had a man in her life. Since Marcus had left the company, and she'd been in financial trouble, she'd had too many problems at work to even think about her personal life.

It hadn't always been like that. Her first year in college she'd fallen madly in love. Tim had been a scholarship student who worked nights to make ends meet. Chloe had thought it terribly romantic the way he struggled to make his dreams come true. She'd given him her virginity one night after they'd seen a foreign film and eaten pizza in his apartment.

It had been young love at its best, but by spring they had already started growing apart. She'd dated lots of guys after that, but none were serious. Then, three years after she and Marcus started their business, she met Paul Monroe at a trade show. He owned an upscale shoe boutique in Philadelphia, he was attractive and they were the same age.

The three of them had hit it off right away. At first it was just business, with Paul and Marcus hatching the idea that Chloe should design on spec a line of shoes that would be less expensive than one-of-a-kind custom shoes, but were still ultra-high quality. Paul would sell them in his store.

She'd resisted the idea, but Marcus had convinced her that it wouldn't be the same as mass production. Eventually she agreed.

She and Paul worked closely on the project, with him advising her about the type of shoes his clients preferred. One thing led to another, and they fell in love. Before she knew it, one minute, he was talking about marriage and, the next, suggesting that she increase the production of shoes. Marcus had pushed at the same time, so Chloe agreed, putting way more capital into the venture than she felt was wise.

As a business deal, it was a total flop. Paul had badly underestimated his clients' willingness to pay top dollar for fine shoes. He was stuck with expensive inventory and she and Marcus had put thousands of dollars into spec shoes that couldn't be sold unless the prices were slashed dramatically. The deal had eaten into their cash reserves, putting them close to the edge. And Chloe's personal relationship with Paul hadn't been strong enough to stand the strain. They broke up.

Since then, Chloe had dated often, but no one had truly touched her heart. Like her friends in the Thursday Night Club, she enjoyed single life. She had her work and her friends to keep her occupied. Her life was good.

But as she looked around Red Rock, seeing people going in and out of shops—mothers with their children in tow, or the older couple who crossed the street just ahead of her and, walking hand in hand, went into a shop—she wondered now if maybe she was missing something.

In New York she'd never given much thought to marrying and having children—at least, she hadn't since she'd broken up with Paul. Yet in the back of her mind she'd always hoped that she'd wind up like her parents someday, meeting Mr. Right and having a close family. Back home, she was so involved in her work that it was easy to forget that dream, but Red Rock seemed to bring it to the fore. It was the sort of place where couples would build a life and a family.

Chloe shook her head. What was happening to her? She'd been in Colorado for barely twenty-four hours and she sounded as if she was ready to pack up her belongings in a covered wagon and head out West for good.

Obviously, it was a case of being enchanted with something that was new and different. Sure, there had to be lots of advantages to living out West in a small town. Cody had found so many that he'd never returned to the East Coast. But there were a hell of a lot more advantages to living in New York, especially for a woman like her, who'd lived in a big city all her life.

Chloe checked her watch. It was still fifteen

minutes before she was due to meet Dax, but there was no reason she couldn't go into the club. Wanda had described Cody's office there, how he had autographed pictures of old movie stars on the walls. She'd love to take a look at them. Besides, she wanted to see where her uncle had worked. Like his office at home, it would help her get a better handle on the man.

She crossed the street and stepped inside both sets of doors. This time when she saw the long mahogany bar with the mirror in the gilt frame over it and the buffalo head squarely over the center of the mirror, she tried to picture her uncle sitting there, talking to his various friends, taking pride in his establishment.

"May I help you?" a brunette with a short pixy haircut asked.

Chloe held out her hand. "Yes. I'm Chloe James, Cody's niece. I'm meeting Dax here in a few minutes, but I thought I'd look around a bit first, if you don't mind."

"Oh, sure thing," the woman said. "I'm Nancy Tyler, and I work the lunches here and the evenings when Wanda is off. Dax was in first thing this morning, but he went to the bank a while ago. If you like, I could give you a tour of the place. Or would you rather be left on your own?"

"Well, I don't want to keep you from your work. But if you could point me in the direction of my uncle's office, and maybe the kitchen, I'd appreciate it."

Nancy grinned. "Sure thing." She turned to the tall man with the beard who was polishing glasses behind the bar. "Jake, this is Miss James, Cody's niece. I'm going in back to show her around. Will you take care of anyone who comes in?"

"No problem. Howdy, Miss James, I saw you here last evening."

Chloe smiled bravely, hoping he hadn't seen her falling into Dax's arms, but knowing he probably had. "Hello, Jake. Nice to meet you, too."

With that, she followed Nancy through the club. As they headed toward the rear dining room and across the dance floor, Chloe tried to gauge her feelings. Did she notice anything special? Magical? She didn't think so. Of course, until the night before, she'd never been in an authentic western bar before, so she found the atmosphere alluring in that sense, but she didn't think that was what Jamie had been talking about.

Chloe continued to follow Nancy down a short hallway to the offices. Before opening the door to Cody's office, the woman showed her the room next to it. It was fairly large, big enough to accommodate a small private dinner party, if necessary. In the center of the room was a large round table where Nancy said some of the guys, including her uncle, had played poker.

"Cody didn't come back here much the last few years, except on Thursday nights when the boys played cards. But Dax hasn't changed a thing."

The walls were lined with photos of movie stars, many of them autographed, just as Wanda had said. In the center of one wall was a picture of a lovely blonde standing between Virginia Mayo and Errol Flynn. The photo was signed, "To Julia from Errol."

"Is that photo of Mrs. Sommers?" she asked.

Nancy went over to the picture. "Yes, and she's in the one over there, with her husband, Hap, and Cody. I think this was taken when the Sommerses celebrated their twenty-fifth anniversary here at the club."

"I guess this has been the site of a lot of parties over the years."

"Oh yes," Nancy said. "Pretty near everyone in town has been to a party at the Cowboy Club one time or another. We've had weddings, lots of birthday parties, anniversary parties. It's everyone's favorite spot."

"Yours, too?" Chloe asked.

"You bet. I met my husband here. I grew up in Red Rock, so I'd been coming to the club for years. Bill was in town to do the wiring for the new motel they built outside of town, the one Dax used to own. I was filling in for Wanda one night. It was a Friday, and I usually don't work Fridays, and Bill came in to ask for a table. He was the best-looking man I'd ever seen, bar none." She began fanning herself. "One look at him, and I was a goner."

Chloe smiled. This was what Jamie had been talking about. It had to be. "And I take it you convinced him to stay in town?"

"You bet I did. There's been enough work to keep him busy. Right now he's helping Dax to renovate the saddlery."

Chloe's eyebrows rose. "Dax owns that, too?"

"Yep."

Chloe was pleased. If Dax had owned the motel, and now owned the saddlery in addition to his half of the Cowboy Club, then he was established enough to be able to pay her a good price for her piece of the club. Assuming Jamie was right that he wanted it, that is.

She moved to the next room, the one that Dax now used as an office. "Did my uncle spend much time here?" she asked.

"Not in this room, no. But if you mean at the club, sure. He came in every day, usually sitting at the end of the bar where he could see the entrance and the dining room. He'd sort of hold forth. Everyone came by to say hello to him. He was real well liked, Miss James."

"Please, call me Chloe. And you don't have to stay with me if you'd rather be out front. I'll just wander around in here, if you don't mind."

Nancy left then, saying to give her a shout if she needed anything. Chloe went over to the desk and picked up a picture of Cody, Dax and three other men sitting around a poker table. One of the guys looked like the cowboy who had fixed her flat tire, Hank or Heath, something like that. All the men in the picture were smiling, except Dax. His expression told her nothing. A true poker face.

Chloe was standing there, holding the photo, when she heard someone clear his throat behind her. She turned and saw Dax. Again, he was dressed in black from head to toe—the toes being encased in a handsome pair of snakeskin cowboy boots that she was certain had set him back a bundle. But for once, Chloe didn't dwell on shoes. Her eyes returned to his. They were a deep blue, even bluer than she remembered when she'd thought of him while trying to go to sleep the night before.

"Oh, hello," she said, pulling herself together. "I wasn't snooping. I just wanted to see where Uncle Cody worked."

Dax stepped over to take the picture from her hand. "You're half owner of the place, Chloe. Feel free to look at anything you like." He studied the photo. "This was taken the night of our first poker get-together. It was Cody's idea that some of the boys meet every Thursday evening for a friendly game. We're still meeting, and every last one of us misses your uncle."

Chloe felt a well of emotion. "Thanks for sharing that. You know, we never even met, but staying in his house, and being in this club, I am getting a sense of the man. I think I would have liked him."

Dax nodded. "You would have. We all did."

"Well," she said, gathering herself, "I don't want to hold things up if you're ready."

"No problem. I've taken the liberty of asking Ben to prepare a sampling of some of our more famous dishes, so you can try them. Then, after lunch, I thought we might drive out to the Lone Eagle Ranch. Julia Sommers is real anxious to meet you. In fact, she would like us to have dinner with them tonight if you're free…"

That made her wonder if Dax and Julia might be planning to buy her out together. But since Dax didn't say anything specific, Chloe didn't either. "I'm at your disposal, for lunch as well as dinner."

He winked. "I might hold you to that."

Despite herself, she blushed. Then, to cover up, she quickly looked down at herself. "But I'll have to change. I can't go to someone's house for dinner dressed like this."

Dax took a good long look at her, starting at the top of her head and ending at her feet. He seemed to stare at her toes for a long, long time. And Chloe was almost sure that she saw the beginning of a smile at the corner of his mouth. "You look fine," he said finally. "But if it's important to you, I'll make sure you have plenty of time to change. Just leave everything to me."

6

HER TOES WERE PINK! Bright pink. Dax tried to be cool as he put his hand at the small of her back to escort her to the booth he'd reserved. It was Julia's favorite, the one she'd been sitting in the evening Hap proposed, and the one Clay had requested when he'd asked Erica Ross to marry him last fall.

Of course, Dax didn't have anything as permanent as a proposal in mind—no way, no how. But the booth had brought luck to both Hap and Clay. Maybe it'd work for him, too. He'd been hearing for years that there was a kind of magic here that made people fall in love. Not that it had ever happened to him, but he'd seen it at work with others.

"Oh," Chloe said, "do we need to monopolize a booth? What if a large party comes in?"

He shrugged. "I don't think it'll be a problem." He stood aside as she slid into the booth. Again he took in her scent. This time she smelled like gardenias. He recognized the flower because the woman in Aspen who owned the fancy ski shop—the brunette he'd had a fling with a couple of years earlier—had used perfume like that. Only he hadn't liked it quite so much on her.

He slid into the booth next to Chloe, not quite as close as the night before but close enough. Nancy approached and put two glasses of water on the table.

"Ben says he's ready whenever you are," the waitress told her.

"Then why not bring out some of the appetizers? And anything Chloe would like to drink."

Chloe asked for iced tea, and Dax stuck with water.

"Did you have a chance to get any of the information I requested?" she asked.

He was a little disappointed that she got right down to business, but he didn't let it show. "Yep. I made copies of the profit-and-loss statements, accounts receivable, tax returns, everything you wanted. You can send them to your accountant whenever you like. I have a fax machine in the rear office."

"Oh, good. I need to fax a design to Carlo, one of my employees, as well. I'm going to make some shoes for Wanda. The poor thing was suffering with those awful heels last night and I designed some shoes that will be much more comfortable for her."

"My, my," he said. "If you do something about Wanda's feet, I don't know what she'll have left to complain about. She moans about those corns of hers more than Cody complained about the folks in town who were against growth."

Her ears perked up. "And is growth an issue?"

"It has been. But even Clay McCormick, Julia's grandson, has come around, and he was the biggest traditionalist of the lot. Julia hired Erica Ross to come to town to do a feasibility study for her ghost town project, and Clay fell in love with Erica. That took care of that."

Chloe chuckled. "Julia must be one hell of a woman."

"Oh, she is. To tell you the truth, I think Cody was more than a little bit in love with her. They were dear friends, very close, though in a very proper way. Cody'd have cut off his legs before he'd ever consider doing something to come between her and Hap, not that it would have done any good. But I think Julia ruined Cody for anyone else."

"I thought Mrs. Sommers was a widow."

"She is. Has been for years. But she's a one-man woman, and I guess your uncle was a one-woman man." He looked up as Nancy returned to the table with a couple of plates. "You'll love Julia. Everyone does."

Nancy put down a dish of snake bites, bits of barbecued snake on fried bread with black-eyed peas, and a second plate loaded with armadillo eggs. "Help yourself."

Chloe gulped, appearing a bit queasy. Dax repressed a smile as she regarded the food, studying it as if she was going to have to take a quiz later. That gave him another chance to observe her, unnoticed. Last night she had struck him as sexy, a little vulnerable and definitely bedraggled. Now Chloe looked every inch the polished New Yorker. Pink toes and all.

There wasn't a woman in all of Red Rock who would come to the Cowboy Club for lunch dressed in fine wool pants and open-toe heels. But in a strange way, Dax liked it that Chloe was different. He dressed differently from the other guys in town, and it had sort of become his trademark. It also made him wonder if maybe he and Chloe were alike in ways that were important. If so, it would be a new experience for him.

"Which one will you try first?" he asked.

"I'm not sure," she said, putting up a brave front. "The buffalo last night was terrific, but I'm not so sure I want to eat snake."

Dax chuckled. "Then try the armadillo eggs. They're really deep-fried cream cheese filled with jalapeño peppers. Whenever Cody had a cold, he ordered some of them. Claimed they cleared up his sinuses pronto."

Chloe grinned. "I'm glad you told me that. This morning, when Jamie helped me get settled in his place, I couldn't help wondering what he had been like. Not that it hadn't crossed my mind before, but being in his home made him seem so much more real."

"Cody was an original. And once you were his friend, well, you were a friend for life." Despite himself, he hadn't been able to keep the sadness out of his voice.

"You really do miss him, don't you?"

Dax nodded, liking it that she understood his feelings without him having to say much. That didn't happen often, though in fairness, it wasn't as though he ever encouraged that kind of intimacy. Which sort of made him wonder why he was doing so now.

He took a sip of water and said, "In ways, he was like a father to me, though he always treated me as an equal. Cody cared about this town. Said he'd never felt at home until he landed in Red Rock. I sort of felt the same. That was a bond between us. We'd both come from someplace else, and we both loved Red Rock. Still, I was surprised when he left most of his property to the community church."

Chloe put her hand on his arm. Dax liked the coolness of her touch. He liked it very much. "Were you upset when Cody didn't leave any of his property to you…or his other friends?" she asked.

Dax shook his head. "Hell, no. None of us needed it. And Cody understood that I took pride in the fact that I'd earned everything I had. He wouldn't have wanted to take that away from me."

Her eyes lit up at his words. She even gave his arm

a squeeze before she let go of him. "I understand. I'm exactly the same."

He felt bereft when she took her hand away. "You are?"

"I started my shoe business with a friend six years ago. To get started, my parents helped me with some of their savings, but I paid them back with interest. Last year I bought out my partner. It's been a struggle, but I had this vision of making one-of-a-kind shoes, and I didn't want to compromise that vision just to be a success."

Dax listened to her, admiring that she had a dream and was willing to do what it took to live it. He'd always marched to a different drummer, as well. But he had also heard what she'd said about her business needing money. If that were so, she'd want to sell her interest of the Cowboy Club for cash...and as quick as she could get it.

Hell! And just when things were going so well.

Without betraying his concern, he picked up one of the armadillo eggs and held it in front of Chloe's mouth. It was an intimate gesture, and by the look in her eye, she had noticed.

"Come on. Have one. They're spicy, but they won't kill you."

She chuckled. "Will the snake?"

"Probably not. Actually it tastes a lot like chicken. It's the idea more than anything."

He popped the appetizer into her mouth. As she chewed, tears came to her eyes. It was all he could do to keep from laughing when she grabbed her water and began gulping it down.

"Dear God, that was hot."

She was fanning her hand in front of her open mouth when he picked up one of the barbecued snake bites and offered it to her. She nodded, so he put it in her mouth, too. For a moment she just sat there, looking as if she couldn't decide whether to eat the thing or spit it out. Then, when she began chewing, her eyes lit up.

"Hey, these are delicious."

"Well, leave room for the tostada salad."

"My God, if I ate like this every day, I'd weigh a ton."

Dax took his napkin and dabbed a bit of barbecue sauce off the corner of her mouth. "I wouldn't worry about your figure, Miss James," he said in a voice so low it was barely above a whisper. "From where I'm sitting, you look just fine. All the way down to your pretty pink toes."

He couldn't fail to notice that she turned bright red. Or that she popped a second armadillo egg into her mouth to avoid talking.

CHLOE WAS ALONE in the back room of the Cowboy Club, sitting at the big desk. In front of her was the information she wanted to fax to Angela. After she and Dax finished their tostada salads and she'd sampled the southwestern chicken, he had asked if she was ready to go over the information she'd requested the night before.

Boy, was she ever. From her perspective, things had gone downhill fast after he fed her the armadillo eggs. Oh, she'd tried to act as if he wasn't getting to her. She'd put up a good front, complimenting him on the quality of the food and trying to ask halfway intelligent questions about the place. But the longer she was around Dax, the stronger his magnetism seemed to get.

So she was relieved when they'd returned to his office and she could hide her expression behind the profit-and-loss statements, the year-to-date information and a summary of the accounts receivable. She had to ask quite a few questions in order to clarify certain entries, but she found that concentrating on the answers was nearly impossible. Dax stood so close to her that she felt his body heat. And when he brushed her arm to point out a certain figure, shivers went down her spine.

She'd been at the point where she was certain he would notice, when Nancy had interrupted to say that Dax had a phone call and he had left the room.

So she'd plopped down in the big chair that her uncle had undoubtedly sat in for years and years, and considered her situation. There was no escaping the fact that she had to take some responsibility for the way things had gone with Dax. In spite of what Jamie had said, Chloe had thrown caution to the wind and chosen to wear the sexiest daytime shoes she'd brought. And when Dax noticed her pink toes, sure, she'd been embarrassed, but she'd also been pleased. She was in no position to complain.

But *why* had she wanted that reaction? That was what baffled her.

For the second time that day, Chloe looked around the room at the various photos. There were movie stars posing with local cowboys and couples holding hands. Everyone seemed a little larger than life— more glamorous, better-looking, happier. Jamie claimed that there was a special mood in the club that people reacted to. Maybe that's what she was feeling. Or maybe the explanation was simpler. Maybe Dax was special, too.

She'd never met a man of the West before, yet the fact that he was a new type for her couldn't explain everything. She had encountered men who were good-looking, occasionally even one or two who were in Dax's league. But they hadn't made her react like this. Once more Chloe ran her laundry list of excuses through her mind: she'd been thinking about Belinda's wedding recently; it had been too long since she'd been involved with a man. Both true.

Still, in the normal course of events, she knew that she'd never even look at him twice—considering that she'd come to Red Rock to do business with him. Since Paul Monroe, all she'd had to do was remind herself that she'd been down that road before and a man who'd looked sexy one minute seemed terribly unappealing the next.

Yet this time, for some unknown reason, she wasn't buying it.

Before she could analyze her feelings further, Dax returned.

"Sorry that took so long, but it was the bank. I deposited last night's receipts just before you got here. The teller called to say she'd put it in the wrong account and she'd take care of it by shifting the funds if I'd tell her again where I wanted the money to go."

"Then everything's okay now?"

"Yes. Are you ready to fax that information to your accountant?"

She nodded. "And I need to send off that design and some instructions to Carlo, as well."

"Good, then as soon as that's done, we can take that tour of the town I promised you."

She agreed and in minutes they were walking through the main dining room and past the bar. Dax's hand was firmly at the small of her back. Chloe felt the warmth of his fingers through her sweater. It made her feel alive, more alive than she'd felt in a long, long time.

Surprisingly, the tension between them seemed to abate somewhat once they stepped outside onto the wooden boardwalk. Wondering why that should be, she turned to Dax. He was as handsome as ever. Tall and sexy. A hunk and a half. Angela would probably give her eye teeth to be spending an afternoon with him, whether they were business partners or not.

"Our first stop should be right across the street, at the newspaper," he said, interrupting her thoughts.

"I've already looked in the window and checked out the latest edition." An amused smile played across her lips. "It's a little different from the *New York Times*."

"Probably more interesting, too," he replied, teasing right back. "But I want you to meet the editor. He's a good friend of mine, and he was close to your uncle, as well."

They crossed the street and went into the building where the *Recorder* was housed. Wiley Cooper greeted them as they came in the door. He looked about forty years old, was tall and dark with black hair that had a little silver at the temples. He was good-looking in a distinguished way, though Chloe didn't think he was as dashing as Dax.

"I'm glad to meet you, Miss James," he said. "I was at the club last night with Heath, and we saw you. But we didn't introduce ourselves since you were otherwise...occupied."

From the twinkle in his eye, she knew Wiley was referring to her tumble into Dax's arms. Knowing that made her want to crawl in a hole all over again, but instead she shook hands with the editor.

"I believe I saw your photograph in my uncle's office. From what I hear, you used to get together for poker on Thursday nights."

Wiley chuckled. "Guilty as charged. Boys will be boys, you know, Ms. James. We do like to have a friendly game every week, though sometimes there's more talking and eating than betting."

"I know how that is. I have a group of women friends who meet in midtown Manhattan every Thursday. We call ourselves the Thursday Night Club for Spinsters, Divorcées and Other Reprobates."

"Now that's a mouthful," Wiley said with a smile. He glanced at Dax.

"You consider yourself a spinster?" Dax asked, the surprise in his voice evident.

Chloe turned to him. "I've never been married, so I qualify. Though to tell you the truth, I think of myself as more of a reprobate." Grinning, she turned to Wiley and added, "And you know how it is... reprobates will be reprobates."

Wiley laughed out loud, slapping his knee. A slow smile crept across Dax's face. Chloe felt wonderful.

They chatted for a few more minutes, though Dax was hardly in the conversation, seemingly more interested in watching her—or perhaps more interested in pondering her reprobate comment than he was in listening to what was being said. Then Wiley took her on a brief tour. The highlight was the antique printing press that was still used to produce the weekly newspaper. Seeing the press, she had a deeper appreciation of why her uncle had loved Red Rock. Though the town had modern conveniences, the past was very much a part of the present.

That was nice. It seemed so solid, so natural. Inviting, in a way. Yet she loved New York with its millions of people and its anonymity. Identity back home came from one's family and friends, or one's career. Here, in Red Rock, it came from one's place in the greater community.

She and Dax thanked Wiley for the tour and then went on, retracing the steps she had taken before lunch.

"Bored yet?" he asked as they waited to cross the street.

"Of course not! Everything's interesting because it's so new to me."

"Just what I wanted to hear."

As they crossed the street, Dax took her hand. It felt so alive it was almost as if she could feel the energy flowing from his fingers to hers. It was like being back in the Cowboy Club all over again.

Why, she wondered, hadn't she ever met someone back home who made her feel this way? Someone nice and convenient. But she already knew the answer. Men like Dax didn't live back East. Cowboys and oilmen and riverboat gamblers were a different breed. They truly *were* a little larger than life. And they were as different from her as New York was from Red Rock.

Chloe knew she shouldn't be holding his hand like this—it only made her want more, and that wasn't wise. So, when they got to the other side of the street, she gently pulled free of his grasp. Dax didn't say a word about it, but she'd have bet her last pair of pumps that he'd felt the electricity as strongly as she had.

She was searching for something to say, some question she could ask to ease the tension, when they came to the saddlery. Dax stopped to look in the window of the old building.

"Have you decided what you're going to do with it yet?" she asked as he cupped his hands around his eyes to better see inside, just as she had earlier.

He turned to her, moving so that his body shadowed her face, she supposed to better read her expression. "How did you know I owned it?" he asked blandly.

"Nancy mentioned it when we were talking before

lunch. Apparently her husband is doing some of the renovation."

Dax nodded. "Yes, he is." He fished in his pocket and pulled out a key. "This is one of the oldest buildings in town. It even predates the Cowboy Club. The brick is all original. Want to see inside?"

"Sure."

Dax opened the door and stepped aside so she could enter. Though there were no traces left of the saddlery, Chloe could smell leather. She took a deep breath, loving the fragrance. It always made her think of the first time her father had taken her to his shop. He had only had one shoe repair shop then, and it was tiny, but to her it had been as wondrous as Santa's workshop. The smell of leather had permeated the room. And there were shoes everywhere— men's leather shoes, ladies' fabric shoes waiting to be dyed to match a special dress, children's shoes in for resoling.

His shop had always seemed like a magic place, and she had known early on that somehow, some way, she would work with shoes. She'd been much older when the notion of actually designing shoes had occurred to her, but even then she had known that she didn't want to work in a studio somewhere, drawing. She wanted to be right in the middle of everything, where she could see her designs literally come to life.

Chloe heard Dax clear his throat and she turned to him, embarrassed at being caught daydreaming.

"Is it like home?" he asked, making her wonder if he was really that good at reading her expressions, or if it was simply a lucky guess.

She nodded. "More than you can imagine. My father owns three shoe repair shops, so I grew up around leather. It's always been a big part of my life."

She peered around, noticing that the floors were wide wood plank with pegs in them. They'd been re-sanded, but not stained or sealed yet.

"Is that how you wound up in the shoe business?" Dax asked.

"Only partly. The other half of the equation is my mother. She's French, and like many Frenchwomen, style and fashion and design are a big part of her life. They've been her career, as well. Mother's the head seamstress for a designer in New York. She makes quite a few of my clothes, too."

Dax stared meaningfully at her pants. Chloe nodded. "Yes, she made these. And I make all of her's and Daddy's shoes. It's a good trade-off, both financially and emotionally. I like wearing clothes she made just for me, and both Dad and Mother like knowing that I made the shoes they wear."

She stepped to the middle of the room, appreciating the proportions of the building. The ceilings were high, as in her loft. An antique white brass light fixture hung in the center of the room.

"That must be nice," Dax said, once more interrupting her examination of the building. "I can tell by the tone of your voice that your parents mean a lot to you."

She nodded. "They do. I'm the only child, so we've always been close. We live not terribly far from each other. I manage to see them once or twice a month for Sunday dinner. Usually for bouillabaisse."

As Chloe spoke, she noticed that Dax was hanging on her every word. Then it hit her. A New Yorker was probably every bit as exotic and strange to Dax as the local cowboys were to her. Once she put it in that context, his interest made complete sense.

"So, was it like that with you?" she asked, deciding it was time to take the focus off herself. "Did you wind up with the Cowboy Club because you had family in the restaurant business?"

Dax leaned against a brick wall and folded his arms over his chest. "Nope. Not even close. In fact, while you were talking, I was thinking how different our childhoods were. I never had a family. My mother wasn't even married when she had me, and she died when I was still a baby. I grew up in an orphanage. At eighteen, when I left there, I took whatever jobs I could to make ends meet while I went to school."

Chloe felt her heart go out to him. He must have experienced a lot of pain and loneliness as a child. How sad. "How did you wind up in Red Rock?" she asked softly.

"Won a piece of land in a poker game. That was my preferred manner of earning a living—gambling. But it was more a means to an end than anything. Anyway, I won the land where the motel is now located, came to Red Rock to sell it and fell in love with the town instead." He looked directly into her eyes and added, "Does that surprise you, Chloe?"

"Yes. But now that I think about it, I suppose it helps me to understand why you and Cody were close, despite the age difference. You both made Red Rock your home after coming from someplace else. And you both were alone in the world."

"Only, Cody had you...and your parents."

Chloe shook her head. "Not really. I never even met him, you know. But I guess family had to mean something to him or he wouldn't have left me his interest in the club. I only wish I'd known him. It might have justified the gift he gave me."

Dax moved closer to her. He reached out and lifted

her chin so that he could look directly into her eyes. Chloe's heart nearly stopped. "Don't waste a minute on regrets. Cody wouldn't have wanted that. Trust me."

She took a slow step back. His hand fell away and her jaw felt warm where his fingers had touched her. "But you were his friend," she said, trying to keep the focus off her reaction to him. "He should have left it to you...or to someone else in town."

"I don't think so. I own half the Cowboy Club and this building, too. And some vacant land outside town, a house I rent out, the one I live in and the building the feed store is in."

Chloe blinked. "You're a real estate baron."

"Not exactly. Now that Cody's gone, it's true that Julia and I are the biggest landowners in town, along with the community church, of course, which got most of Cody's property. But the real money around here is in the ranches. Some of the spreads are worth millions of dollars. Clay McCormick owns the Lone Eagle where we're going tonight. He's one of the richest men around. I'm small potatoes by comparison."

Chloe didn't reply. But in spite of the attraction she felt, she hadn't missed the point that if Dax owned all of that, he had to be wealthy—at least on paper. Yet he had downplayed what he owned, which meant that the man was either modest or didn't want her to get the idea that he was rolling in dough.

Again, she looked around the saddlery. "So, what do you plan to do with this place once it's been renovated?"

Dax shrugged. "I haven't decided. It would make a great restaurant, with the brick walls and all. It could be an adjunct to the Cowboy Club, sort of a huge private dining room that I could rent out for special occasions. It's not quite as big as the Elk's Club, but it has more atmosphere."

"Are there enough large parties around here to justify that kind of use?"

"No. That's the problem."

"Then why did you buy it?"

"Because I loved the building." He unfolded his arms and ran his hand over the rough surface of the brick wall. "I guess I liked knowing that this place had been a part of the town for years and years. And my owning it, well, it makes me more a part of Red Rock, too."

Chloe heard real reverence in his voice. And she understood exactly the way he felt, because she'd always had a desire to be a part of something bigger than herself, too. Not many people did.

She'd asked Paul once if he ever felt that kind of need. He'd laughed, saying all he needed was a deal that would make him rich. Chloe had laughed with him, but with time she realized that even if their deal hadn't soured, they wouldn't have been happy. At a fundamental level, they didn't connect.

But with Dax, she did feel a connection—one that went to her core. That was odd, because in a lot of ways they couldn't have been more different. Which made her wonder if being alike on the surface was important. She had always thought it was. Now she wasn't so sure.

7

WHEN SHE GOT BACK to Cody's, Chloe decided to lie down for a few minutes. She was still tired from her long drive the day before, and besides, it would be another few minutes before Angela would be home. She wanted to call her to confirm that the fax had arrived and also to discuss the situation.

So she'd changed clothes, putting on her emerald green silk wrap over her bra and panties, and had a glass of juice. Then she'd plopped down on the bed, staring at the old pine armoire across the room and thinking about Dax. The last thing she'd expected when she'd planned this trip was to meet someone like Dax Charboneau. It was still early in their relationship, and she was probably projecting, but she was beginning to wonder if maybe he might be the kind of guy who could touch her soul as well as turn her on.

His remark about needing to be a part of the town had sure gotten to her. Of course, the difference between them was that Dax had found what he wanted to be a part—of Red Rock and the Cowboy Club. As much as Chloe liked her career, she couldn't honestly say that she had found that special something that she wanted to connect with—that something that was bigger than herself. She wondered if she ever would.

Probably all she needed was to talk to Angela to ground herself. God knew, back home she never worried about these sorts of things, she was too busy trying to keep her company afloat. Which was why she ought to keep her mind on business now.

With that in mind, she picked up the old-fashioned black phone on the bedstand next to her and dialed her friend. Angela answered on the second ring. "I thought I'd better report in, kiddo."

Angela chuckled. "How are the cowboys?"

"The local boys are okay." Chloe paused for a second. "In fact, more than okay."

"Oh? Do tell. But give me a minute to pour a glass of wine first. I have a feeling this may be a doozy."

As soon as Angela was back on the phone again, Chloe launched into the story, starting with her flat tire and ending with lunch at the Cowboy Club and the fact that she and Dax were going to Julia's place for dinner that evening.

"Well, well, well," Angela said. "I take it this means you'll be coming home with a thrilling story about romance in the Old West."

"No way. Angela, you know how I feel about mixing business with pleasure. I only told you how good-looking Dax is because I thought you'd be interested in what the men out here are like."

"I see...you were just giving me a sociological overview, is that it?"

"Very funny."

Angela chuckled. "Honestly, Chloe, I don't know what your problem is. Or maybe I do—Paul. But you can't let him affect the rest of your life."

"Mixing business and pleasure is dumb and you know it."

"Yeah, well, tell it to Belinda. If she hadn't mixed a little business with pleasure, she wouldn't be marrying Charles. And if I recall correctly, Pam and Grayson worked in the same law firm. And Liz and

Colby owned some oil rights together. Need I go on?"

"This is different."

"How?" Angela sighed audibly. "Chloe, its not like you're going to move to Red Rock and start running the restaurant with him. Under those circumstances, I agree that the romance might take a header when you wanted to put fillet of sole on the menu and he wanted to keep the chicken-fried steak."

"More like the buffalo and snake."

Angela choked on her wine. "The what?"

"Snake. It's on the menu, along with buffalo stew. They're really quite good. You'll have to try them sometime."

"Good God," Angela said. "Chloe, don't view this as a business trip. It's more like traveling to another universe and being the representative from earth. My advice is...do a little exploring, and then come home to tell the rest of us all about life in the Old West."

"But what if it screws up my deal to sell the club?" she wailed.

"How could it? Look, even if you do have the slimmest ankles east of the Hudson, chances are you aren't going to make Mr. Wonderful want to buy the club if he has already decided he isn't interested. And if he is, well, maybe he'll be less likely to try to take advantage of you if he likes you. The bottom line is, you're equals here. You both own half the club. I'll be going over the information you faxed me tonight and then I'll talk to you again tomorrow. After that, you'll have a much better idea where you stand."

Chloe had to admit that plan sounded reasonable.

"Good," Angela said. "Then while I'm slaving over these figures, you go have a nice time. How often do you get to go out with a guy like Dax? Or to dine at the home of an ex-starlet who actually knew John Wayne and Errol Flynn? This is an adventure. Something to tell your grandkids about when you're eighty-five."

"Okay. You've convinced me. I'll do it for my grandkids."

Angela laughed. "Do it, and you just might end up having grandkids."

CHLOE WAS in a sound sleep when she was awakened by the sound of knocking. She blinked, disoriented. Where was she? Oh, yes, in Red Rock at her uncle Cody's house. Then she looked at her watch and saw that it was nearly five o'clock. Dax! He had told her he'd pick her up around five to take her to dinner at Julia Sommers's house.

Chloe bounded out of bed as the sound of knocking started again. Looking down at herself, she saw that she was barely presentable—she had on the thin emerald green silk robe over her bra and panties. Cinching the silk belt tight around her waist, she went to the living room, which was directly off Cody's bedroom, and opened the front door.

Dax stood there, his fist raised as if he was just about to knock again. The sight of him nearly took her breath away. He was all in black again, with a western-cut shirt and a bolo tie under a black suede jacket. And he had on a black cowboy hat. He looked both wicked and sexy.

"I'm so sorry," she said. "Please come in. I must have fallen asleep." She stepped aside so he could enter.

Dax took off his hat as he came in the door. She caught a whiff of his cologne. "No problem. You go on and change. I'm sure Julia won't mind if we're a little late."

"I'll hurry. It'll only take me a minute." She watched as he put his hat on top of a low bookcase and plopped down in one of the big leather chairs. He seemed very much at home. "Can I get you anything?"

He shook his head. "You go on. I know where everything is, so don't worry."

Chloe excused herself and went to the bedroom, carefully closing the door. There was no lock on it—not that she needed one, she was sure. Still, it felt strange knowing that Dax would be just on the other side of that door while she was changing. But she'd already made them late, so she couldn't dwell on that point. Fortunately, she'd already decided what to wear.

Jamie had said that Julia liked to dress up. Bangles and beads were definitely her style, so for once Chloe didn't have to worry about her clothes. Her mother had made her a fabulous deep purple satin cheongsam with a mandarin collar and cap sleeves. The dress was perfectly plain except for a slit up the side of her thigh.

Shortly after her mother made the dress, Chloe had come across a fairly large piece of antique brocade. It was the same shade of purple as the dress and it had golden dragons embroidered on it. Her mother had made her a long narrow stole and there'd still been enough fabric left over for shoes and a purse.

Chloe had designed platform sandals with a wide strip of the fabric across her toes and an ankle strap that was a bit wider than what she usually made for herself. But she'd wanted to balance the wide strap over her toes with the chunky platform heel. The result had been stunning. And by using slightly wider straps, the gold dragons were clearly visible. Carlo had also made her an envelope purse.

She'd worn the outfit to Belinda's engagement party and everyone had raved over it. With her fair skin, emerald eyes and dark hair, jewel colors suited her. And the combination of the plain dress with the more elaborate stole, shoes and bag was a knockout.

Of course, the stole might be a bit too much for Red Rock, but it could get cool in the evening, even in the spring. Besides, Jamie had counseled her to be herself and not try to change her style simply to fit in. It was good advice, and Chloe knew it.

She slipped out of her robe, and quickly put on a purple lace bra and matching panties. After shoes, lingerie was her big weakness. She absolutely loved matching the color of her panties and bras to her outfits. And her mother, who shared that weakness, indulged her big time, giving her expensive French lingerie sets for her birthday and Christmas.

As she reached for her panty hose, she caught a glimpse of herself in the mirror. What would Dax think of this outfit? she wondered. She shivered at the thought of him seeing her in her bra and panties, knowing he'd approve. It was oddly sexy to think he was in the next room, sitting in the chair that faced the door separating them.

She sat down on the edge of the bed to put on her panty hose, wondering why she suddenly felt free to have these thoughts. Angela's call. That was the explanation. Chloe had been struggling hard to keep things with Dax on a professional plane, and all she needed was one tiny conversation with her friend to let all her emotions hang out. Obviously, she'd wanted to be talked into letting go, giving herself permission to have a little fun. But why did it have to be now?

Chloe finished pulling on her panty hose. She grabbed her dress from the hanger on the back of the bathroom door and slipped it over her head. As the satin slithered over her hips, she ran her fingers over the fabric. It was smooth, sensuous.

Chloe reached back to zip the dress. The zipper started just above her waist and went to her neck. She was able to zip it without a problem, but she couldn't seem to get the hooks at the top. She backed up to the mirror and turned this way and that to see what the problem was, but she couldn't tell.

Knowing she'd have to get Dax to help, she put on her shoes, buckling the ankle straps, then went to the bathroom to check her makeup. She put on a bit more mascara and lined her lips in bright pink. Then she put some spicy oriental perfume behind her ears and on each wrist.

Grabbing her purse, she put both her perfume and lipstick inside. She was all set. She took a deep breath, picked up her stole and opened the door.

Dax immediately got to his feet. He gave a low whistle. "You look great."

She glanced down at herself. "You don't think it's too much?"

He shook his head. "Nope. Julia doesn't believe in too much."

"And what about you?" she challenged.

"I think too much on anyone else is just right on you."

Chloe felt her heart lurch at the words and she gave him a smile to indicate that she appreciated the compliment. Then she remembered the hooks. "Oh, I nearly forgot. I had a slight problem with my hooks. Could you help?"

As she turned her back to him, Chloe felt Dax move close. She felt his breath on her neck and the warmth of his fingers as he pulled her hair aside.

"This will only take a second," he said. She felt his fingertips brush the back of her neck as he fastened the two hooks. Then his hands rested on her shoulders. "All done," he said lightly.

Chloe took a deep breath before turning to face him. The electricity between them was so strong, she almost hoped he would take her in his arms and kiss her. At least that would end the awful tension. At least then she would know.

But as she turned, Dax removed his hands from her shoulders. She looked up and saw a gleam in his eye. It was almost as if he'd read her thoughts. Or maybe, it was that he'd been thinking the same thing himself.

FROM THE MOMENT that Julia Sommers greeted them at the door in her electric blue silk caftan that was heavily embroidered with silver, Chloe started to relax. She wouldn't stick out like a sore thumb, after all.

Chloe quickly glanced at Julia's feet and saw that she had on fancy silver sandals that had huge fake gems embedded on the heels and across the toe strap. Julia was as flamboyant as Jamie and Wanda had indicated.

"Welcome to the Lone Eagle," Julia said, beaming. "I am so pleased to have you here. And you're even more beautiful than the pictures Cody showed me."

"Oh, thank you. You're very kind," Chloe said.

"Not at all." Julia took a step back to take her in. "Your outfit is absolutely fabulous. Those dragons are to die for, as my granddaughter Kiley would say."

Chloe thanked her again, and then Julia turned to Dax to say that Clay and Quentin Starr, her other dinner guest, were in the barn, checking out a new horse Clay had recently acquired.

"I suppose that means I ought to go out there and see if the animal is up to snuff," Dax said, giving Julia a wink.

The older woman pinched his cheek. "That's what I like about you, Dax. You don't have to be hit on the head." She chuckled. "So, go. Erica and I want to get to know Chloe, maybe have a little girl talk about the wedding."

"You don't have to ask me twice," he said. "I'm out of here."

Chloe watched, amused, as he gave Julia a peck on the cheek and then headed out the front door. If only she could handle the man half so easily, Chloe thought. But then, Julia had the advantages of both age and experience.

When the door clicked shut, Julia turned to her. "I'm so happy to finally meet you, my dear. You are absolutely stunning."

"Thank you. I was worried that it might be too much…"

"Nonsense. Wear what you like and let the others drool or laugh…whichever they want. That's my philosophy."

Chloe heaved a sigh of relief. "That's kind of what Jamie Cole told me. That I should be myself and not worry."

"Good advice for anyone," Julia said. Then, taking Chloe's arm and starting down the hall, she went on, "I've heard so much about you from Cody, my dear. My only regret is that he isn't with us tonight."

"I feel like that, too," Chloe said. "But I know he would appreciate you inviting me. It is so kind."

"It's always good to meet a new friend. Speaking of which, I want to show you the house because I hope you'll feel at home here…and come back again."

They passed oil paintings and tile floors—the mood was sort of Spanish, sort of western. But when they came to the sunroom at the back of the house, it was filled with plants and lighter colors. This was clearly Julia's lair.

"Please, make yourself comfortable, and I'll have Rosita bring us something to drink. Erica will be joining us in a few minutes. When I left her, she was still trying on some of the shoes we ordered for the wedding. Unfortunately, nothing so far seems to go with her dress."

Chloe grinned. "I know how that is. A friend of mine is getting married soon and I just gave her the shoes I designed for the occasion. She's going to wear a very simple bias-cut satin dress and she needed something that would complement it without stealing the show."

"Well, this is a similar problem. To my delight, Erica's going to wear my wedding gown, which is practically an antique at this point. It's a period dress and the shoes these days all seem to have the wrong look to go with it."

"Can I help? As a minimum, I might be able to steer her in the right direction."

Julia seemed relieved. "To tell you the truth, I was hoping you'd volunteer. I knew from Cody you were in the business, but I didn't want to impose."

"No problem. In fact, I'd love it."

"Excuse me, *señora*," a middle-aged Mexican woman said from the doorway, "but have you decided what I should bring you?"

Julia turned to her. "Chloe, this is Rosita. She runs

the place and without her I'd have pulled my hair out years ago."

"Glad to meet you, Rosita."

"Me, too, *señorita*. Your uncle was a very nice man. Most kind to everyone."

"Thanks," Chloe said.

"Will you join me in a cocktail, dear?" Julia asked. "Erica has a liver problem and doesn't drink...and, well, I don't like to drink alone."

Chloe agreed. When Julia told her that the housekeeper was famous for her margaritas, they decided that would be perfect. They'd have their drinks after they finished checking out the shoe situation in Erica's room.

As Julia led the way down the long hallway, the older woman kept turning her head to speak. "I can't tell you how pleased I am to finally meet you, dear. Cody showed me your picture each Christmas when your mother sent her annual letter. He was quite proud of you."

Chloe sighed. "Before coming here, I had no idea he cared so much. If I had, I'd have made more of an effort to get to know him. We never even met and I do feel guilty about that, especially when he was so generous to me."

Julia stopped, turned around and took Chloe's hand. "Don't feel guilty, dear. I knew Cody for ages, and believe me, he could have visited back East if he'd wanted to. Lordy, he certainly could have afforded it. But with him, I think the idea was maybe as important as the actual thing. He was happy knowing you were close to your parents and running your own business."

Chloe took the opportunity to ask something that had been on her mind ever since she'd seen the photos in Cody's house, next to his rolltop desk. "Do you think he left me the Cowboy Club because he was hoping I'd fall in love with the town, too? Maybe stay here like he did?"

Julia shook her head. "No. He wasn't the type to give gifts with strings, or to try to play God. I do think he'd be pleased that you came out to see Red Rock, though. This town meant the world to him. And the Cowboy Club, well, it was his heart. But I don't think for a minute that he was trying to get you into the restaurant business." She paused dramatically. "And I don't believe he would turn over in his grave if you sold it, either."

Chloe was relieved, though she wasn't sure what to make of Julia's last statement. Was she interested in buying back into the club herself, or was she simply trying to relieve her of the burden of feeling an obligation? Time would tell.

They continued down the hall. The last door on the right was open and a lovely woman with chin-length light brown hair and pale blue eyes was sitting at the foot of the bed. She was wearing a beige silk sheath with a string of pearls and pearl studs. And she was holding her foot up in the air to get a better look at the white satin pump with a lace bow on the toe. When they came into the room, she quickly slipped off the shoe and stood.

"You must be Chloe," she said with a smile, holding out her hand. "I'm Erica. And as you can see, I'm having a bit of a problem." She gestured to the bed that was covered with shoe boxes, some open with shoes spilling out.

"But for a good reason, I hear. You're getting married."

Erica's smile lit up her face. "In three weeks. At least, I am if I can find the right shoes. Of course, the way I feel about Clay, I'd walk down the aisle barefoot if I had to."

Chloe looked at the shoes spread out over the bed. "I take it style is more of an issue than fit?"

"Oh yes. Nothing seems right."

Chloe picked up a shoe and looked it over. It was expensive, an imported well-known brand, and very attractive.

"Is that the dress?" she asked, seeing a full-length clear clothes bag hooked over the door.

"Yes." Julia went over and began unzipping the bag so that she could take out the gown. "The dress was made by Adrian, a famous Hollywood designer back in the forties. I was a particular favorite of his— mainly because he designed so many clothes for Rita Hayworth, and she absolutely hated to go in for fittings." Julia freed the gown from the bag and held it in front of her. "Back then we were almost the same size, if you can imagine, so as a favor to Adrian I would stand in for her. He was most grateful, and when Hap and I decided to marry, Adrian asked if he could design the dress as his gift to me. Of course, I was thrilled."

The wedding dress was so beautiful it nearly took Chloe's breath away. It was chiffon and very romantic, with see-through sleeves, a fitted bodice and full skirt. There was a small collar and a string tie at the neck, but the top of the dress was also see-through, though there was a satin under bodice that covered the breasts. What made the gown really stand out was the color. The top of the dress was cream lightly tinged blush, but from the waist down the color got progressively pinker.

Chloe lifted the hem and found there were six underskirts, all chiffon, each hand-painted to subtly bring more and more color into the dress. The hem itself was almost mauve. She turned to Erica, taking in the woman's soft brown hair and pink cheeks. She would look like an angel in the dress.

"The shoes I've tried so far are all wrong," Erica lamented. "Even if I had them dyed, I don't think they would work. They're just too modern."

Julia hung the dress on the back of the door and went to the bed. She had to move a couple of shoe boxes to make room to sit down. "What would you suggest, Chloe?"

"Well, for starters, shoes in the late forties often had platforms, sort of what I have on now," she said, holding up her foot for them to see the brocade sandals with the golden dragon on them.

"Those are fabulous, Chloe," Erica said. "I've never seen anything like them."

She grinned. "Good, then we're on the same page with the platform idea. So I'd go with that, only with a lower platform than these. They should probably have an open toe, with the narrow V-cut instead of the wider open-toe that came in later. And a strap over the top of the instep rather than the ankle. A soft pinky-mauve that goes with the deepest tone of the dress might be best."

Julia popped up off the bed. "Back in a minute," she said, then rushed out of the room.

"She's such a dear to offer to let me wear her dress," Erica said when her future grandmother-in-law had gone. "Her only daughter never wanted to wear it, and Kiley, that's Clay's sister, doesn't seem to be in any kind of hurry to tie the knot."

"Where is she?"

"London, acting in a play."

"I'm impressed," Chloe said.

"Me, too. Even though I'm from Denver, I'm still a Colorado girl."

"But a city girl, nonetheless…at least, compared to Red Rock."

"Yes." Erica laughed, putting a hank of hair behind her ear. "And it was a problem at first, I can tell you that. I couldn't imagine falling for a cowboy. In fact, I joked to my friend Sally that was the last kind of man I'd even have a fling with." She sighed blissfully. "Clay proved me wrong."

Chloe heard the love in her voice and wondered if she could ever feel that way about anyone. "But don't you feel like a fish out of water here after Denver?"

Erica shrugged. "I did at first. But when I started meeting people, and everyone was so friendly and welcoming, I realized I wasn't all that different. Colorado is home to individuals, some rugged, some smoother. Julia was from Hollywood, but she found a way to fit in here. I'm in the process of doing so. And Clay makes it all worthwhile."

"Not that he wasn't a little slow catching on," Julia said, apparently having heard the last exchange as she was coming down the hall. She was carrying a pair of dusky pink satin shoes very much like the ones Chloe had described. "Sort of had to be hit over the head with a two-by-four, which is essentially what Erica did when she went back to Denver." Julia gave Chloe a sly smile. "Not at all like Dax. Now, that man doesn't need encouragement from anyone."

"Oh?" Chloe said, though she knew exactly what Julia meant.

"You must have noticed, dear, because I don't believe for a minute that Dax is slipping." Julia fanned herself. "That man has had every woman in three counties after him."

"Were you going to show your wedding shoes to

Chloe?'' Erica asked, getting back to the subject at hand.

"Yep. Adrian designed them, too." She handed them to Chloe, who examined them.

"These are very close to what I had in mind."

"Could you make something like that for me?" Erica asked. "I know custom shoes are expensive, but thanks to Julia I'm not paying for the dress, and I've about run out of options."

Chloe smiled. "Sure, but first let me look at your feet. There might have to be some design changes from this one to accommodate your arch. And you want to be comfortable or else you won't be able to dance in them."

As Erica sat down on the bed and took off her shoe, Chloe set to work. But in the back of her mind, she couldn't help thinking about Julia's comment about Dax. He was fast on the uptake, all right. Probably too fast for his own good.

But then, the real question was whether or not Dax was too fast for *her.*

8

DAX HEADED toward the barn, only half resenting that Julia had practically kicked him out. Not that he was all that interested in hearing a bunch of female talk about the wedding, but then, he wasn't too interested in seeing Clay's latest horse, either.

If he had his druthers, which he didn't, his first choice would be to take Chloe and drive straight back to Cody's and spend the rest of the evening making love with her. Not that he didn't enjoy his friends, but the woman was driving him crazy.

Her answering the door in that green silky robe that was the same color as her eyes had about been the last straw. Knowing that she probably had on little or nothing under it had sent his blood pressure soaring. It had taken all his willpower not to pick her up and carry her into the bedroom and make love to her.

Dax sighed. Damn. He really was starting to sound like Clay. If he wasn't careful, next he'd be trying to figure out a way to keep Chloe in Red Rock...at least until whatever it was that they had between them had burned itself out. And he had a feeling that might take a while.

But he was stuck. For the next few hours at least, he'd have to act like a gracious guest. Which meant he'd better stop thinking about Chloe.

With that in mind, he had to admit that Julia had managed to pique his curiosity when she'd announced that Quentin Starr would join them. Dax hadn't known that the guy was even back in Red Rock, which proved once more how preoccupied he was with Chloe. Normally, he'd have been among the first to hear news like that.

Though Quentin had been a Red Rock native, he'd left for Texas fifteen years earlier to make his fortune as a wildcatter. He'd struck oil about the same time Dax had come to Colorado. They'd met then. Good old Quentin had put on a show, the prodigal son home for a visit and spreading his money around like honey on biscuits. Not that he had needed the dough to make an impression. At six-five and with thick browny-blond hair, Quentin Starr had the kind of bad-boy looks that stood out in a crowd and always seemed to appeal to the fairer sex.

About a year ago, Dax had run into him again. By then, Quentin had learned how to handle his wealth. Dax wondered why he was back now. He didn't have to wait long for the answer because when he joined the others in the barn, they shook hands and Clay immediately announced that Quentin was investing heavily in Julia's project.

"How'd you even hear about it? Or is what's happening in Red Rock these days big news down in Texas?" Dax teased.

"Not yet, though that could change if Julia and I get the theme park on the map," Quentin said. "But to answer your question, I heard about it from some of the boys. I keep in touch with Heath, and with John MacInnes. John told me about Julia's plan. He knew I was cash heavy and suggested I might be interested in investing in it."

The words *cash heavy* rang in Dax's ears. God knew, that was one problem he would like to have.

"Are you going to take an active interest in Julia's project?"

"You bet. In fact, I'm all but decided to move back here permanently. I never did like putting my money into something and then not being around to watch it develop, sort of nurture it along. Seeing a town grow and prosper is more my style."

"Yes, I know how that is," Dax said noncommittally.

"By the way, I told Quentin that Cody had passed on," Clay said, pushing his dark brown hair off his forehead. "Said his niece might be interested in selling her share of the Cowboy Club, but I wasn't sure if you were after it yourself or if you had another partner lined up to step in."

Dax could have killed Clay for opening his big mouth. But all he said was, "Well, we're pretty much in the early stages. She only got here yesterday so she's still getting a feel for the situation and I'm looking at my options, too."

"I'll bet you are. Word around town is that she's a real looker," Quentin said with a grin.

Dax scratched his ear. "I guess you'll have to judge that for yourself."

"I wouldn't want to step on your toes," Quentin said. "In business, or personally."

Dax smiled confidently. "I'll be pursuing my own interests, you can be sure of that."

"I wouldn't be out of line to ask a few questions, then?"

"Hey, it's a free country."

"Your share of the club's not on the market, is it?" Quentin asked.

"I never say never, but I figure I'll end up like Cody...hanging on to the Cowboy Club until they carry me out to boot hill and put me in the ground."

Clay ran his hand over the flank of his horse. "Sounds to me like you'd like to buy her out yourself, Dax."

He smiled at Clay, wishing to hell his friend would mind his own business. It'd be one thing if he had Quentin's capital, it was another knowing that the only way he'd ever get total control of the Cowboy Club would be if Chloe was willing to take some sort of a creative deal.

Just his luck that someone with cash to burn would come along and plant his size twelves right in the middle of his pie. But Dax knew that the real question was whether Quentin would want to buy out Chloe even knowing he'd have no chance of getting full ownership. Dax didn't think he would, though he wouldn't want to bet on it.

Being partners with someone was a delicate thing. He and Cody had gotten along just fine. In fact, the last few years, when Cody's health was failing, the older man had given him an extra couple of grand a month for handling all the business. And if Chloe kept her share of the club as a passive investor, he imagined he'd be able to work out a similar arrangement with her.

Cody had once told him that Julia had been a perfect partner. Her areas of interest in the club had been different from Cody's so they hadn't clashed. But Dax and Starr were too much alike. Starr, too, was a take-charge sort of guy. He'd want to run things, and Dax had no intention of sharing control.

Which meant, of course, that he was caught between a rock and a hard place. If he didn't cut a deal with Chloe—and pronto—Quentin might move in on him and buy out her interest himself. But the last thing Dax wanted right now was to discuss business with Chloe. He'd much rather be using his energy to seduce her.

Dax groaned. There had to be a way to get both the girl and the Cowboy Club. There had to be.

His reverie was broken when Quentin suggested that they watch Clay take the new horse for a walk around the corral. Dax had spent some time around horses, but nothing like Clay. Even Quentin, who'd lived in town growing up, had done enough ranch work summers to become more knowledgeable about livestock than Dax. Since the horse talk bored him, he thought about Chloe again.

He'd known a lot of women but he'd never seen anyone remotely like her before. It wasn't just that she was beautiful, or had guts. Something about her essence, her style, got to him. One of the first things he'd noticed about her were those red shoes with the ankle straps. They were sexy and daring and he'd wondered if she was sexy and daring, too.

Then for lunch she'd worn those open-toed shoes that seemed to say to him, "Look at me, I'm not all business." Tonight she'd gone all out. Other than in a magazine about movie stars, he'd never seen an outfit like the one she wore. That Oriental dress should have been all wrong, yet on Chloe it worked. And the purple shoes with the little gold dragons really turned him on. They were wild and different, like the lady herself. Which was probably why he was so hung up on her. A big part of him was like that, too. And the thought of being with a woman who could relate to him on that level was new. Best of all, it was coming at a time when he thought he'd seen and done it all.

Finally, Clay suggested that they join the women inside the main house. Dax was glad. He'd been thinking about Chloe long enough. He wanted to see her.

When they entered the sunroom, Dax saw that both Julia and Chloe were looking at a painting while sipping one of Rosita's famous margaritas. Erica spotted them first. She rushed up to Clay and hugged him. "Oh, I'm so happy. Chloe has saved me. Come thank her, darling, because she's agreed to make shoes to go with my wedding dress. You won't have to marry a barefoot bride, after all."

Smiling, Clay turned and took Chloe's hand in both of his. Dax could tell by the expression on his friend's face that, in love with Erica or not, he was very aware of how gorgeous Chloe was. "Welcome to the Lone Eagle Ranch. We're glad to have you. And if you've ended the great shoe controversy, I'm eternally grateful to you, as well."

Chloe chuckled. "No problem. It will be my pleasure."

"She's already making shoes for Wanda," Dax said. "If she keeps at it, Chloe will have the entire town buying from her."

"I don't think so," Chloe replied, still laughing. "I've seen an awful lot of cowgirl boots in town, and I don't think too many of the women of Red Rock are ready to turn them in for pumps."

"You might be surprised," Julia said. "Besides, there's no reason you couldn't make cowgirl boots, is there?"

"Or cowboy boots, for that matter," Quentin Starr interjected.

Chloe turned to Starr. "Well, that would be a first."

He moved close to her and held out his hand. Chloe took it. "I'm Quentin Starr, by the way. And I'm sure you could make a mean pair of boots if you put your mind to it. Nothing folks in this part of the country appreciate as much as a fine pair of hand-made boots. Could be a business opportunity there, ma'am."

"Thanks," Chloe said as she pulled her hand away from his. "I'll keep that in mind."

Dax liked it that she didn't seem too eager to keep holding on to Quentin. But his relief ended when Quentin took a step closer to her and said, "Dax and Clay tell me you own half the Cowboy Club now."

"I do indeed."

"Well, perhaps we can talk about that sometime." The words were spoken softly, but Dax heard them. And it burned him. Not that Quentin had mischief in mind, but he never ignored an opportunity.

Rosita entered the room then with a fresh tray of margaritas. Both Quentin and Dax took one. Clay, like Erica, stuck with fruit juice. With his drink in hand, Dax moved next to Chloe and casually put an arm around her shoulder. She leaned back into him, and he liked that. Then, speaking to Quentin, Dax said, "I was telling Chloe on the drive over here that we expect your theme park to be a real kicker to the local economy. Don't know how to thank you and Julia."

Quentin's mouth bent into a thin smile. "I do what I can."

"But truly, Dax, *we* should be thanking *you*," Julia said. "One of the main reasons Quentin and I are so enthusiastic about long-term prospects for the theme park is that Red Rock itself is so special. And Lord knows, the Cowboy Club should be high on the list of tourist attractions."

"Thanks, Julia," Dax said, removing his arm from Chloe's shoulders. "But a lot of the credit for that goes to you and Cody. You nurtured it for years."

"I think we all want the same thing for Red Rock, and that's prosperity." Julia looked at each of the men in turn. "This is a big country. There's room for everybody."

Dax noticed that Chloe had listened to the byplay, but he doubted that she picked up on the subtle messages. When there was a lull in the conversation, she deftly changed the subject to Clay and Erica's wedding. Dax wasn't sure if she'd done that because she didn't want to discuss business, or if Starr had already given her more than enough ideas. Either way, it could mean trouble for him.

After a few minutes Rosita returned with a tray of hors d'oeuvres. Dax took one and, after holding it in front of Chloe's lips until she nodded, he popped it into her mouth. He liked the way her lips curved into a smile that promised more. Almost as much as he liked knowing that Quentin had probably seen them.

But then he noticed that Chloe had a look in her eye that said she knew something was afoot. That was okay, too. As long as she was the one who was kept guessing, he'd have the advantage. Of course, with Quentin in the mix now, that could change. But no matter what, Dax had tonight to make his case. And he had every intention of making the most of it.

AFTER DINNER, Clay suggested that they might want to go outside for a short stroll. It was cool out, but not too cool, and there was a full moon. Erica had immediately said that she liked the idea, but Julia had suggested that this might be a good opportunity for her to have a chat with Quentin. Which left Chloe partnered with Dax.

He got up from the table and came around to her side to help her up. She smiled her thanks.

"So, shall we join Erica and Clay?" he asked.

"Yes. But I want to get my stole first."

Dax went off to ask Rosita where she'd put it and Chloe headed for the front door. Erica and Clay were already waiting. Erica had put on a white cashmere cardigan. Clay was wearing a jacket.

"You two go on, if you want. I'll wait here for Dax," she said, seeing that Clay and Erica were eager to be alone.

"Sure you don't mind?" Erica said.

"Not at all."

Clay took Erica's hand and they went out the front door. As Chloe watched them, she wondered if she'd ever feel that way about a man—absolutely sure that he was the one she wanted to spend the rest of her life with.

Her father had known that feeling as soon as he'd seen her mother. And they had been very happy. Their only regret was that they hadn't had more children. But the three of them had been close...and still were. In fact, Chloe suspected that her dad would have already retired and moved away from New York except for the fact that he and her mother didn't want to leave her.

"I finally found it," Dax said, breaking her reverie. "I couldn't find Rosita so I started hunting. She'd draped it over the back of a chair in the living room."

"Thanks."

Dax held the stole open and Chloe turned so he could place it around her shoulders. Then, putting his arm around her, they went outside. The air was fresh and clear and not too cool, and when she looked up, she saw a million stars scattered around the full moon.

"Guess you don't see a sky like this in New York City," he said, giving her shoulder a squeeze.

"No. But once in a while, if I'm out in the country,

in Connecticut, for example, there will be a night something like this." They started down the long driveway. Erica and Clay weren't in sight.

"And what's in Connecticut?" he asked.

"Nothing in particular. But the parents of a good friend of mine live there, and I went there for the weekend not long ago, for my friend's engagement party."

"Oh, I see." Dax stopped and turned to her. "Does it seem like everyone you know is getting married?"

She laughed. "Well, sometimes. Does it seem like that to you?"

Dax hesitated, then started walking again. "I never thought about it much…I mean, until now. Clay was the last guy I thought would ever want to tie the knot. But now he's marrying Erica."

"Do you feel left out?" she asked, chuckling.

"No. More like there's some kind of joke and I don't get the punch line."

Chloe didn't say anything to that, but she was curious as to what Dax meant. There had been genuine doubt in his voice. Surely he understood why people married—everyone did, didn't they? She turned to him and, despite herself, asked, "What is it you don't get?"

He stopped walking and turned to her again. "I don't know. That you would want to stay with one person forever, I guess."

"I see. Well," Chloe said, "you understand why someone would want to stay in one place forever, don't you? Instead of wandering all over the world, I mean."

"Oh, sure. I felt that way when I first saw Red Rock."

"Well, Dax, I guess wanting someone special to spend your life with is sort of like that."

He didn't say anything. But there was enough moonlight for her to see his face. The shadows made him look more dramatic, and she couldn't quite see the expression in his eyes, but she knew by the way he stood there that something she'd said had gotten to him.

Finally, he reached out and cupped her jaw in his palm. "You know, Chloe, you are a very special lady. Cody did me a real good turn when he brought you into my life."

She parted her lips to speak, but there were no words. The stars and the moon and Dax had filled the moment, and breaking the silence didn't seem right. Dax must have felt that way, too, because instead of speaking, he leaned down and kissed her.

At first his lips were so gentle that the kiss was almost like a whisper. But Chloe leaned into it, wanting more, and Dax responded instantly. He put his arm around her and pulled her close as his lips crushed hers.

She gave herself up to him, opening her lips, running her tongue across his teeth before slipping it into his mouth. Dax responded by thrusting his leg between hers. His thigh pressed against her intimately, increasing her desire.

Chloe was beginning to think she'd never get enough of him, even if they stood there until the stars grew cold. But then, Dax moved away from her lips to nibble her ear. His warm breath on her shell, and his moist tongue, drove her wild. If they hadn't been standing out in the open, she would have started unbuttoning his shirt.

Finally, after what seemed like an eternity, Dax pulled away from her and stepped back. Chloe immediately felt cold. Worse, she felt alone, bereft. When she gazed into Dax's eyes, she thought he might be feeling that way, too, though it was hard to tell with the dappled moonlight.

"Maybe I had better take you home now," he said simply.

She nodded. "Yes. Maybe you had better."

He took her hand and held it all the way back to the ranch house. But Chloe knew that what they shared didn't end here—it couldn't. She'd felt the power of their attraction and so had Dax. The only real question was what they would do about it.

After they said their goodbyes to everyone, they got into Dax's Bronco for the long ride back to town. Dax asked if she liked jazz, and when she told him she did, he put on a CD of love songs by Marion McPartland.

They drove in silence, holding hands and listening to the music. By the time they were on the outskirts of Red Rock, Chloe knew that she wanted to spend the night with him. She'd carefully gone over all the reasons why she shouldn't, but in truth she did not believe a one of them.

Dax was right for her—at least, he was right for her while she was in Red Rock. She also knew this wasn't a spur-of-the-moment decision. It had been building from the first moment she'd seen him at the Cowboy Club. And in a way she did not understand, and could not explain, even to herself, she felt that they belonged together.

Soon she saw that they were on the edge of town. In minutes Dax had parked the Bronco in front of her house, just behind her rental car. He came around to help her out of the vehicle and they walked hand in hand to the front door.

Chloe opened her purse and handed Dax the key. He unlocked the door and reached inside to turn on the light. She stepped in and turned to him. "Would you like some coffee?"

"Sure," he said. "I know where everything is. I'll fix it. You just relax."

He tossed his jacket on the couch then went into the kitchen. She heard him rattling around as she put her purse on the bookshelf and draped her stole over the back of an old cracked green-leather chair. Then she sat down on the couch and unbuckled her shoes. She was just setting them on the floor in front of the couch when Dax came into the room. He sat down next to her, staring at her shoes.

"Coffee will be ready soon," he said. Then, nodding toward her shoes, "Do custom shoes hurt your feet, too?"

She laughed. "No. But I usually take off my shoes when I get home. It's just a habit, I guess. My mother had light beige carpeting...and she wanted to keep it light beige."

Dax picked up one of her shoes and held it in his hand, looking it over carefully. "It really is beautiful. Kind of like a painting."

She was touched. "Thank you."

He turned to her then, and when Chloe looked into his eyes she saw the same kind of longing she felt. She swallowed hard, almost afraid to breathe. She didn't want to say or do anything to break the mood.

"You're beautiful, too," he murmured, putting the shoe down and reaching over to caress her cheek. "Maybe too beautiful."

He put his hand behind her neck and drew her closer. They kissed, softly, almost with reverence. But after only one kiss, Dax pulled back. "I better not do that again, because if I do, I don't think I'll be able to stop."

"I don't want you to stop," she whispered.

Dax didn't need a second invitation. He pulled her onto his lap and began kissing her until she was breathless. And when his hand rubbed a nipple through her dress she moaned with desire, wanting him.

He finally pulled away from her and stood up. When he held his hand out to hers, Chloe took it. She stood up and put her arms around his neck and kissed his chin. Then she turned her back to him. "I'll need help with the hooks," she said simply.

Dax unhooked the dress, then slowly unzipped it. Chloe took a deep breath, then turned and let the dress come off her shoulders. The garment slid down her hips and she stepped out of it. She stood before him in her purple lace bra and panties.

"My God," was all Dax said. But he kept his eyes on hers as he unbuttoned his shirt and shrugged out of it, tossing it on the couch by his jacket. Next he sat down to take off his boots, which he carefully placed beside her shoes.

He scooped her into his arms then and strode into the bedroom, where he gently laid her down on the bed. He lay down himself, half beside her, half over her. His thigh was between hers. She squeezed her legs and felt the most delicious sensation.

Dax began kissing her neck and ear. His hand caressed her nipple through the lace of her bra. She strained against him, increasing the pressure of his leg against her mound, knowing she wouldn't be able to get enough of him until he was inside her.

The lamp was still on in the living room, and there was enough ambient light for her to see the dark mat of hair that covered his chest. Chloe ran her hands over his taut muscles, reveling in the hardness.

He helped her out of her bra and panties, then

stood up to get out of his pants. Chloe watched him undress, liking the way the muted light highlighted his torso. His face was obscured by a shadow and she couldn't read his expression, but he seemed to be searching for something.

"What are you doing?" she asked.

"I have to protect you."

She realized that he was getting a condom. But the way he'd phrased it, that he wanted to protect her, filled her with longing.

Dax got back on the bed, gathering her into his arms. She luxuriated in the feel of his flesh. They kissed once, very deeply, and then he surprised her by scooting to the foot of the bed and nibbling on her foot.

Chloe lay back as he kissed her ankle and toes. She'd never felt anything so sensuous in her life. But more than that, she felt as if Dax was truly worshiping her body, making love to her and with her. Soon he began nibbling her other leg, slowly moving up her calf to the inside of her thigh. Chloe felt a rush of desire. And when he lightly flicked his tongue at the inside of her thigh, she grabbed the bedspread with her fists and clenched her teeth.

He teased her for what seemed like an eternity before his tongue touched her feminine lips. She thought she would explode right then. Closing her eyes, she lost herself in the sensation. When she felt the first pulse of her orgasm, Dax pulled away and placed his palm over her, applying just enough pressure to keep her on the edge but not enough to make her reach her peak. She had not known that anyone could have such control over her body.

After a moment, she calmed down. Dax stood then and pulled her around so that she was crosswise on the mattress, her hips on the edge of the bed, her feet dangling to the floor. He grabbed a pillow and stuffed it under her hips. Then, lifting her legs to his shoulders, he pressed his sex against her opening.

Chloe was so ready, both emotionally and physically, that she was as wet as she had ever been. Dax eased into her and began thrusting, plunging a little deeper, moving a little faster each time. She felt consumed—with him, with the moment. In a way, she did not think she could ever get enough, and yet in another way, she felt as if she was rushing toward something she had to have, no matter what the cost. She was so excited that she shook her head from side to side, moaning, crying, wanting more, always more, yet knowing that they wouldn't be able to keep up the pace for long.

Then, with a shuddering cry, they both went over the edge.

It was a long time before Dax lowered her legs and eased out of her. Then he stretched out beside her and gathered her close. Her head was on his chest and she could feel his heart. His skin was warm and fragrant. She was breathing hard. But she didn't care about that; she didn't care about anything except this feeling of…completion. Her skin tingled. Never had she felt so alive.

Vaguely she wondered if that meant anything. Was Dax the most accomplished man she'd ever made love with? Or was what they had truly special? Or was it simply that she was coming into her own as a woman? She didn't know…and she didn't want to analyze it—not now. It was enough to enjoy, to savor the moment.

They both fell into a silence. It was a long time before Dax finally spoke. "That was perfect," he whispered. "I don't think it gets any better than that."

"I'm sure of it." She sighed. Then she rolled over

so that her back was to him. He immediately snuggled up to her and cupped her breast. They lay like that for a long time, with Dax occasionally caressing her leg or kissing her neck. After a while, Chloe felt him harden against her. "Mmm," she said. "Does that mean what I think it means?"

"Well, it does if that's what you want."

She told him it was, but in her heart of hearts she wondered if it could possibly be as special as the first time. But she surprised herself. Her hunger was soon as great as it had been before. Almost at once, she wanted him again, but Dax took his time, giving her pleasure then pausing long enough for her to stay in control without quite losing the edge of her desire. When he finally parted her thighs and entered her from behind, Chloe was more than ready for him.

He moved slowly, with one hand caressing her nub at the place where he entered her. Time and again he paused so as to prolong their lovemaking. She was sure they could go on like that forever.

But she was wrong.

Even knowing that moving faster would bring them to climax, they both seemed to sense that they could hold back no longer. And when they finally exploded, Chloe knew she wouldn't trade this experience for anything in the world. Being with Dax, making love with him, was simply something she had to do. The only unknown was whether he felt the same.

9

DAX QUIETLY got out of bed, picked up his briefs and black jeans and padded out of the room in bare feet. Chloe was sleeping peacefully and he didn't want to wake her. As he got to the living room, he put on his pants. It was 4:00 a.m. and he hadn't slept. What a night! He couldn't decide if he was the luckiest man on earth or the biggest damn fool alive.

And all because of a woman. A very special woman.

He sat down in Cody's favorite chair, the one he'd sat in by the hour when Dax had come over to shoot the breeze with him. Cody had always listened patiently, taking an occasional sip of bourbon as Dax laid out his plans for the Cowboy Club. God, how he missed that man.

But Cody was gone and Dax was dealing with his friend's niece—if you could call it dealing, that is. Why had he made love to her? Why couldn't he have waited, at least until they had come to some sort of understanding about the club? Now if he told her that he wanted to buy her out but that he had to have terms to do it, she'd think that he'd made love with her just to gain a business advantage.

Damn. Damn. Damn.

And all because he had no control. Disgusted with himself, Dax knew that he hadn't been able to resist her from the minute Chloe had fallen into his arms and he'd seen the challenge in her eyes.

At lunch in the club, when he'd fed her hors d'oeuvres, it had seemed like the sexiest thing he had ever done with a woman. She'd felt it, too. He was sure of it. Even holding her hand had been sexy.

Dax leaned back in the chair and closed his eyes as he relived their lovemaking. Was there any way he could have held back once he kissed her? He didn't think so. He had wanted her as much as he'd ever wanted a woman. And when they made love, he felt as if he was eighteen again.

After the second time, they'd taken a shower. Of course, they had gotten turned on all over again as they rubbed soap over each other. When Chloe had taken his sex in her slippery hand and began soaping him, it was all he could do to wait until they had dried off before he was taking her to bed again.

For him, the last time had been the best. He'd had more control so he'd been able to fully enjoy Chloe's pleasure. He'd never forget the look on her beautiful shadowed face when she climaxed. She had curled up in his arms then and fallen asleep almost at once.

But he hadn't been able to relax. He was too keyed up.

Dax got up and went to the kitchen. The coffeepot was still plugged in. He threw out the coffee, cleaned the pot and got it ready for morning. Then he went back to the living room and opened the cabinet where Cody had kept his liquor. Sure enough, it was still there. He gave Jamie a silent thanks and took down the bottle of whiskey. Pouring a couple of fingers of amber liquid into a glass, he sat down, this time in the old cracked green leather chair across from Cody's.

Chloe had draped her stole over the back of the chair. Dax fingered it. Then, as he stared across the room, he noticed the way his boots were next to her shoes with the little gold dragons on them.

Why was she so special to him? he wondered. And even more important, why should it matter?

If Cody was there now, what would he advise? Dax knew the old boy would no doubt tell him to get on with it. But what did that mean? Sure, he could do what he had to do to cut a deal over the club, but he might wind up losing Chloe in the process. And he knew already that he wouldn't like that. Besides, as soon as Chloe sold her interest in the Cowboy Club, she would no longer have an excuse to stay in Red Rock. Which probably meant that he should do nothing for the present.

His problem hadn't changed. He wanted Chloe and he wanted the club. It was that simple. And it was that complicated.

But what if he couldn't find a way to have both? Now that he'd made love with her, which would he sacrifice?

He took a sip of whiskey, liking the feel of the burn as it slid down his throat. If this was a hand of poker, what were the odds that he'd end up with both the woman and the club? Dax figured it was sort of like drawing one card for an inside straight—not good. Chloe was a New Yorker. She had her own life and business back there. Why would she stick around in Red Rock just to play with him?

Dax realized he was starting to sound like a lovesick schoolboy. Hell, he'd never worried about how long something might last before. What was the big deal? It would last as long as it lasted. And if this was all they'd have, then so be it.

But even as he rolled the words through his mind, Dax knew there was something about Chloe that made him want more—more of her, more of what they'd shared. Satisfied that he at least knew what he wanted, Dax drained his glass. A big part of him wanted to lie down next to her again. Even if he didn't fall asleep, the idea of having her near him was appealing.

But it would be better if he left now. Not that Red Rock was full of vicious gossips or anything, but if word got around that his Bronco had been parked in front of her place all night, there was bound to be talk. No, he'd leave her a note, inviting her to dinner at his place. Yes, that was a good idea. He wanted her to see his house anyway. For some reason, he was real curious what she'd think of it.

WHEN CHLOE WOKE UP it was just after six. She turned over, expecting to see Dax, but he wasn't there. Instead she found a note saying that he thought it was best to leave before the neighbors woke up and saw that his Bronco had been there all night. He also said that he wanted her to come to his place for dinner that evening.

Chloe clutched the note to her breast, smiling. It was sweet the way Dax wanted to protect her. It said volumes about him as a man—and also about Red Rock. In New York, no one would have noticed, or cared, who she spent the night with. There was an advantage to that, of course, but the downside was the knowledge that you didn't matter enough for anyone to wonder what happened to you.

She got out of bed and went to the bathroom where she put on her robe. Seeing the wet towels on the floor, she thought about the shower she and Dax had taken after they'd made love the second time. Talk about erotic! Even now she could almost feel the way his sex had felt alive in her hand as she soaped him. He had come close to taking her right then and there.

Chloe smiled as she regarded her image in the mirror. Practically no sleep to speak of but she looked great. Rosy cheeks. A smile on her face. She brushed her teeth, thinking about that. In truth, she didn't have anything to smile about. Oh sure, she'd had the best sex ever with Dax Charboneau, but she had also managed to complicate her life. On the other hand, maybe the problem wasn't as big as she thought. Maybe, if Angela was right, it was her attitude. She sure hoped so.

She spent the next couple of hours puttering around the house. She made her bed and straightened up after she ate breakfast. Finding the coffeepot ready to be plugged in was another bonus. Dax must have gotten it ready for her before he left. Again his thoughtfulness touched her.

Sitting at the little table in the kitchen, she got out a pad and pencil and played with some ideas for shoes. Since coming to Colorado, Chloe had seen an awful lot of cowgirl boots, and though she couldn't say she thought they were wonderful, there were elements about them that intrigued her, especially the ones with heavy tooling on the leather.

Quickly sketching, she designed pumps in a rich cordovan leather. With tooling they would look especially good with pants. One of her clients in Chicago, a real estate broker, would love them, she was sure.

She was working on the design for a pair of low boots that also had tooling in the leather when she got a call from Julia Sommers. Chloe thanked her for the lovely dinner the night before, and then they got down to the reason for Julia's call.

"I didn't say anything about it last night since you

were busy with Erica, but is there any chance that you'd be willing to make some shoes for me?"

Chloe laughed. "Of course. That's what I'm in business for."

"Good. Because I very much would like to take advantage of your being in town so we can talk face-to-face. I've taken the liberty of phoning a couple of friends about you. Edris Peeler, Judge Peeler's wife, is so interested in seeing you she wants to drive over from Cortez. Bernice Bender would like to meet you, too. Both women love shoes and can well afford yours."

"I'd be delighted to meet them," Chloe said.

"Good. Then if you're free, why don't we meet for lunch at the Elk's Club? This is the day the Rotarians get together at the Cowboy Club, so it will be real crowded."

"That sounds fine. I'd like to see the Elk's Club anyway."

"I'll make arrangements for noon then. It might also be a good idea if you brought some of your shoes with you. I know everyone would love to see them."

Chloe agreed, and then she spent the remainder of the morning working on the design and measurements for Erica's shoes. Her plan was to drop by the Cowboy Club and fax the design to Carlo on the way to her lunch date with Julia.

By eleven she put away her sketch pad so that she could dress. She took a quick shower and then had to decide what to wear. She'd packed three suits, in addition to the one that was ruined, but they might be too businesslike. She decided on the taupe silk pants.

She'd brought an off-white silk sweater with cap sleeves and a jewel neck. She could wear it with the slacks and carry the navy jacket to one of her suits. It was a classic blazer style and would go okay. Which left her with her usual problem—which shoes to wear.

Chloe didn't like wearing dark shoes with light pants, so that left her with two pairs of taupe shoes to choose from. One was a classic spectator in taupe and navy. It would go great with the outfit, and spectators were perfect for spring, but somehow the look seemed a little formal for Red Rock. Her other choice was a T-strap in pale taupe kid that had very high heels. She'd brought them to wear with one of her suits.

First she tried on one shoe, then the other. In New York, it wouldn't have taken her five seconds to decide—she'd have gone with the spectator. Then Jamie's advice came back to her. She would be herself. Last night she'd dressed outrageously by Red Rock standards and nothing horrible had happened. To the contrary, she'd gotten lots of compliments and Dax had loved it.

She'd be herself today, as well.

At a quarter to twelve, Chloe entered the Cowboy Club to fax her designs to Carlo. Nancy greeted her at the door, telling her that Dax had a meeting with someone in Cortez that day. Chloe was disappointed, since she'd hoped to see him, but she reminded herself that they'd be together in a few hours.

After she finished faxing, she returned to her car and drove to the Elk's Club. It was only a short distance away, but she'd packed one of each pair of shoes she had with her, as Julia suggested, and she didn't want to drag her suitcase through town, wheels or no.

Julia greeted her just inside the entrance and ushered her toward the private dining room at the rear of the building. "I hope you don't mind, dear, but my little party seems to have grown. Erica decided to come along, and then several of the other women heard about it, and well..."

Julia opened the double doors into the rear banquet room. There was a horseshoe table and over a dozen women were standing around talking. Wanda was there. Chloe also saw Erica and Jamie Cole. Julia introduced her to the others.

"I know everyone is dying to see the shoes. Do you think we could set them out on that table by the wall and everyone could look at them while we wait for our lunch? I've taken the liberty of ordering Caesar salads with grilled chicken for all of us."

"Sure," Chloe said. "And I'll be glad to describe the process of making custom shoes, if everyone is interested."

"That would be wonderful," an older woman with silver hair said. "I'm Edris Peeler, and I have a feeling you and I are going to do a lot of business together. I've never seen a pair of shoes I didn't like."

"Just my kind of customer," Chloe said, smiling. Then she turned to Jamie. "I didn't expect to see you here."

The tall redhead grinned. "I know, I told you how frugal I am. But I've been thinking about those beautiful silver shoes of yours. Not that I'd order anything quite that frivolous—I don't have anyplace to wear them. But I could use an all-purpose shoe that would work on Sundays, for services and weddings. My old heels have about had it, and my foot is so long and narrow I have a hard time finding something that fits."

"Don't worry. That won't be a problem."

Jamie and Erica helped her to set out the shoes. The women quickly began looking them over. Her purple sandals and the silver shoes were particular favorites, though Erica homed in on the red-ankle-strap ones she'd worn the night she met Dax.

Jamie held up the sandals with the little gold dragons on them. "Can't you just see me in something like these?" she said, grinning.

"I don't think anyone would listen to a word of your sermon," Wanda said. "They'd be too busy watching your feet."

"You've got that right," Erica said, chiming in. "And you certainly couldn't wear them to my wedding…no one would look at me."

The women all laughed and Chloe turned to answer a question from Bernice Bender, who wanted to know if she could get shoes in a certain shade of blue.

"Of course," Chloe said. "Usually my customers send me a swatch of fabric if they want me to make shoes for a special outfit. But if you don't have extra fabric, and you can't cut off a tiny piece from one of the seams or the hem, you can always go to a paint store, get a paint chip that matches and send it along. One of my customers has been doing that for years…but then her husband owns a chain of paint stores in Dayton."

"Oh my," one of the women said. "Do you have to own a chain of paint stores to afford custom-made shoes?"

Chloe had explained that the shoes were expensive—outrageously expensive by most standards—partly because they were handmade and very labor intensive, but also because she used high-quality leathers and fabrics and trims.

"But I'm getting mine free," Wanda declared with a smug smile. "Because I work for her."

"To tell you the truth, Wanda," Julia said drolly, "my guess is that the whole town would've chipped in for a pair if it would make you stop complaining about those corns of yours."

"And my bunions," Wanda said, teasing right back. "Don't forget my bunions, Julia."

The waiter interrupted to say that they were ready to serve lunch. Everyone sat down, with Chloe in the center of the horseshoe. Wanda sat on one side of her and Julia on the other.

As she ate, Chloe answered questions about the most expensive shoes she'd ever made—evening shoes with real gold heels encrusted with diamonds for the wife of a Middle Eastern sheik. And the most outrageous—shoes designed to look like gondolas for a ball in Venice. They had been worn by a man!

Chloe was having a good time, as well as doing a little business, but every so often she'd check her watch and think about Dax. In only a few more hours she would see him again. Part of her was a little nervous about that. It was always awkward seeing someone the first time after you'd made love.

She was also concerned that the business deal still was between them. After lunch, she would call Angela and they could discuss the information she had faxed her. Not only did Chloe need to know where she stood financially, but the time had come to ask Dax straight out what his intentions were. If he didn't want to buy her out, she might as well know so she could start pursuing other buyers. Maybe Quentin Starr.

That would undoubtedly be best for the romance anyway. Not that this would turn out to be a serious relationship—she'd be returning to New York as soon as she made a deal, and Dax had to be aware of that.

Chloe sighed. So much for being in and out of Red Rock in a New York minute.

BY THE TIME Chloe got back to her uncle Cody's house it was nearly four. She had sold fourteen pairs of shoes, four each to Edris Peeler and Julia, who also ordered a pair of red heels similar to the ones Chloe had, as a birthday present for Erica.

Jamie had wanted basic black pumps. Chloe had gotten a terrific deal on quality leather that had been embossed to look like crocodile. Using it would cut sharply into her profit, but Jamie had been so kind to her, she felt it was the least she could do.

As soon as she got home and put away her shoes, Chloe called Angela.

"The good news is that the Cowboy Club does a terrific business and has a very healthy cash flow," the accountant began.

"And the bad news?"

"With a quarter-of-a-million-dollar loan on the building, there isn't much chance a bank will give you another loan against the business. You'll have to sell if you want to get any money out of the place."

"What loan? I looked over the documentation and didn't see anything."

"For the kitchen remodeling. It was clearly marked, kiddo. I don't know how you missed it."

Chloe did. She'd been so distracted by Dax's presence that she hadn't seen it. Some businesswoman she was! "What do you suggest I do next, Angela?"

"I'd get an updated appraisal on the business and building. The bank ought to be able to steer you in the right direction."

"I can see the banker tomorrow. Anything else?"

"Well, it might be a good idea to find out what your options are as far as buyers are concerned. Is Dax interested or not?"

Chloe admitted that he hadn't said anything about

it. Which reinforced her belief that they had avoided the issue long enough.

She hung up then and went to the bathroom to freshen up. Looking in the mirror after she brushed her teeth and fixed her makeup, Chloe decided the jacket was a little businesslike, but if it turned cool she'd need it. Besides, she'd be talking business tonight, at least for part of the time. Even so, she decided to change her shoes. The T-strap heels were so much sexier than the spectators, and she didn't think the evening would be *all* business. At least, she hoped it wouldn't be.

Thirty minutes later, after stopping by the grocery store to pick up a chilled bottle of Chardonnay, she was on her way to Dax's house. It was located just a couple of miles outside of town, on a twenty-acre parcel of land.

When she parked the rental car in the circular driveway, Chloe got out of the car and looked around. Dax's house was a modern rancher, made of stucco. It was much bigger and more elegant than she'd expected. It was on a hill high enough to have a perspective of the nearby mountains and the distinctive red rocks.

Dax opened the front door and started toward her before she was halfway to the house. As soon as he reached her, he pulled her into his arms and kissed her, hard. "I've been thinking about that all day," he murmured. Then he leaned over to kiss her again. "Good morning." He kissed her a third time. "Good afternoon."

She pulled back, laughing. "No, you can't kiss me good evening. The sun hasn't set."

He pinched her chin playfully. "It will. Come on in. I want to show you everything."

They walked arm in arm up to the house. Dax took

the bottle of wine from her, thanked her, then set it on an antique table in the entry hall. There was a huge mirror over it that also looked like an antique. Both pieces appeared to be Spanish, though Chloe was no expert.

The house was beautiful. Dax had always liked antiques, he told her. As a young man in New Orleans, he'd spent his spare time wandering around the city's many antique shops where he'd developed a taste for fine-quality furniture. And when he came across a piece he couldn't resist, he'd bought it. Many of the things in his house had been stored for nearly a decade before he finally had a house to put them in.

"Then this is your dream home," she said, looking around. It was very masculine, with strong browns and taupes and a smattering of bright blue.

"Yep. I bought the land about three years ago because I loved the view," he said, showing her the flagstone patio that could be accessed from the living and dining room as well as the master bedroom.

As they finished the tour, Dax asked what she thought of the place. "Well, it is beautiful. And unusual. I've never seen a house so large that had only one bedroom, unless you want to count the den."

"That's what the builder said, too. But my friends are right here in Red Rock. I don't have a family, so what would I need a guest room for?"

Chloe didn't say anything, but the fact that his dream home only had one bedroom told her a lot. Apparently Dax didn't even consider the possibility of sharing his life with a woman and children. Family wasn't part of his game plan.

Not that it should matter to her. They both knew this would only last as long as she was in town. But it made her feel a little sad for Dax. He didn't have a clue as to what he was missing.

They went out onto the flagstone patio. There was a table with four chairs and a bright blue market umbrella. The barbecue was brick, built into a low wall that separated the patio from the spa. Dax got the Chardonnay from the entry hall where he'd left it. Then he opened the bottle, poured some into a glass and handed it to her.

"How about a toast to the Cowboy Club?" she said.

He lifted a eyebrow. "It brought us together, so why not?"

They each took a sip of wine, then Dax smoothly took her glass from her and set it on the table. He indicated that they should both sit. "We need to talk about business." He paused dramatically. "I take responsibility for not bringing it up sooner. I'd planned to yesterday but then we sort of got sidetracked—not that it wasn't delightful."

She smiled.

"But in the middle of the night, it started bothering me that I hadn't told you that I wanted to buy out your interest in the club...assuming you still want to sell."

"I do." Chloe took a deep breath. "Of course, we will have to agree on a price. And if Julia and Quentin Starr are correct, and Red Rock is on the verge of booming, then I think that should be factored into the equation."

Dax rubbed his chin. "I don't have a problem with that in theory. But it is kind of speculative. Tell you what, you come up with a formula that seems fair, and I'll agree to it."

Chloe didn't say anything for a moment. On the surface it seemed that Dax was cooperating, but he might be stalling. Because he wanted her to stay in Red Rock or for some other reason? She didn't know, and in any case she couldn't complain that he was being unfair. The burden to come up with a formula was on her shoulders. It would be up to her to present a proposal in a timely fashion.

She decided to agree to a sale in principle for now. Tomorrow she would talk to the bank and get the ball rolling with appraisals and so forth. Dax seemed relieved with her decision. He handed her the glass of wine, and this time he suggested that they toast each other.

Chloe agreed. After taking a sip, she said, "So, what have you planned for dinner? More snake and buffalo, or have you killed a coyote in my honor?"

He chuckled. "Nothing so exotic. Just chicken. I thought I'd barbecue that and some corn. And I can make us a spinach salad, too."

She watched as he got the coals ready, liking the fluid way he moved. Dax told her he'd made his own barbecue sauce and the chicken had been marinating since that morning. The recipe was a variation of one he had tried in New Orleans and it had a bite to it.

By the time dinner was ready, the sun was setting and it was too cool for them to eat out, so Chloe set the dining-room table while Dax brought in the food. The meal was delicious. Afterward, Dax served good strong coffee with chicory. That was a particular favorite of his, he told her. He had developed a taste for it growing up in New Orleans.

"You'd love the Big Easy," he said to her as they sat in the dining room with its wall of glass. It afforded a panoramic view of the sunset that seemed to make the red rocks glow with an inner fire. A single fat vanilla candle sat on the round dining-room table. "There is a charm, a lazy decadence about the place, that gets to you."

Chloe put down her coffee cup and smiled. "And

what is it that you think would appeal to me…the charm or the decadence?"

"Both."

"And why is that?"

"I don't know. Because they appeal to me, I guess." He stared at the flickering candle as if trying to gather his thoughts. Chloe could tell he was taking her question seriously. "I think there is something…offbeat, maybe…about both of us. We're each willing to take risks to live our dreams. Most people are afraid to do that."

Chloe understood what he was trying to say, but she wasn't sure what that meant for them, professionally or personally. She didn't think he knew what it meant, either. But she didn't ask any more questions. Instead, she sipped coffee and enjoyed the silence and the candlelight.

She liked the way the flickering candle shadowed his face. It reminded her of the night before, when he'd undressed in the shadowy light from the lamp in the living room. Dax must have been thinking about that, too, because he took her hand and kissed it. Then he led her to the living room. They sat on the big taupe suede couch and listened to jazz as they sipped the last of their wine.

They talked for hours, discussing everything from their childhoods to their dreams for the future. In the back of her mind, Chloe was very aware that they would be making love later, but neither of them seemed to be in a hurry. Instead, they savored the moment.

Chloe liked it that Dax understood her desire to build her own company and run it her way. Similarly, she understood why Dax wanted to buy her out. It wasn't a selfish need to own the entire pie—he truly cared about how the Cowboy Club was run, and he wanted to preserve its place in the community. Also, he wasn't too keen on the notion of taking on a new partner who might want to change that.

That had led them to a long discussion about partnership. Chloe had talked about Marcus and how there had always been underlying tension between them because he had wanted the company to go in a different direction.

"Then you were relieved when he left?" Dax asked.

"Yes and no. It was nice to have someone to share the burdens with...I suppose that is the benefit of having the right partner."

"I know what you mean. Cody and I used to talk about the club by the hour. I was real lucky that the last couple of years he let me handle most decisions. He knew his health couldn't take the stress. Of course, it helped that we wanted the same thing."

That had made Chloe wonder. If she hadn't needed the money from the club for her business, could she and Dax have worked together, as partners? She didn't think so. He had his ideas, and if she got involved in the restaurant business, the time would surely come when she'd have ideas of her own on how to run things, and not necessarily the same way he wanted.

Dax was right. They were alike in that they marched to different drummers than most people, but it remained to be seen whether the drummer they marched to was the same.

Once she'd figured that out, Chloe understood why Dax was so cooperative—if she sold to someone else, he'd be forced to deal with a partner he might not want. That was leverage she could use to get him to meet her price, but Chloe didn't want to think it might come to that. Still, she tucked the idea into the back of her mind. That way, if she had to use it, it would be an available option.

But even as she told herself that, a little voice inside her asked if she'd have the guts to do whatever it took. Her mind and her heart had never been at odds like this before. It made her wonder if there was any way on earth she could manage to satisfy both needs, or if she was doomed to failure.

10

CHLOE SPENT the next two days trying to meet Dax's challenge. But it soon became apparent that the fact that the town was on the verge of a boom could not easily be translated into a formula. Even so, she had to see a lot of people just to get the information Angela wanted.

Ford Lewis was tied up in court over at the county seat, so Chloe started with the bank. The manager agreed that an updated appraisal was a good idea. Unfortunately, the only appraiser around wouldn't be able to get to the job for a few days.

At first that annoyed her. Then she realized that she had to meet with Ford Lewis anyway. Besides, being in Red Rock was no hardship. It wasn't costing anything to stay at Cody's, and her business wasn't suffering. To the contrary, when she wasn't trying to schedule meetings with bankers, lawyers and appraisers, she was sketching ideas for the shoes she'd sold at the luncheon.

Chloe had come up with designs for Jamie Cole and Julia right away. She met with both women to show them her sketches. Jamie was thrilled and didn't want her to change a thing. Julia wanted a different look for the evening shoes. Chloe made the necessary alteration and faxed the finished designs to Carlo.

Chloe also took Wanda out to lunch one day to thank her again for having taken her in, and she met

Jamie for coffee. But the nights were reserved for Dax.

They were together every evening, having dinner and then making love until the small hours. Two nights in a row she slept at his house, and he'd had dinner with her at Cody's and then stayed with her the night before, though he left before dawn.

By mutual consent they talked about everything but business during those times. Still, pleasant as being with him was, she knew she had to hold back to protect her feelings since there was no chance that it could lead anywhere. Even if they didn't live thousands of miles apart, there was a fundamental difference that couldn't be overcome—family, commitment and a future that included children was important to Chloe.

She'd forgotten that dream during the years she'd struggled to keep her business afloat. Having good friends had also made it easy to put those desires on the back burner. But being with Dax, knowing that they connected in so many fundamental ways, made her yearn for a relationship where she could truly share her life with someone, as her parents shared their life.

Chloe figured that wasn't likely to happen. It wasn't that Dax was a womanizer, though he was obviously popular with women—very popular, from what Julia had said. It was more like Dax didn't truly understand why having a family was important. Having been an orphan, he didn't realize what he was missing. Chloe figured the chances of that changing were not good.

Still, she hadn't come to Red Rock with the intention of finding Mr. Right. She had met a sexy man and she was having fun. That was more than she could say for the past six months of her life. The wise thing would be to enjoy what she had.

Unfortunately, she didn't always do the wise thing.

DAX SAT at his desk in the back room of the Cowboy Club, shuffling papers until it was time to go see Ford Lewis. Yesterday he'd gotten into trouble with the lawyer. Ford was in the difficult position of trying to be Dax's friend and Chloe's lawyer. And though Dax should have realized that everyone was wearing too many hats—trying to maintain friendships while doing business—he had tried to ask his old buddy a few hypothetical questions. Ford had immediately told him in no uncertain terms that, hypothetical or not, Dax was asking things he couldn't discuss, seeing as how he was representing Cody's estate.

Dax had been embarrassed for having thoughtlessly put Ford in an awkward position. He'd apologized at once.

"Don't feel bad," Ford had said. "This is hard on all of us. Besides, it's sort of business as usual for me. Being the only practicing lawyer around has its disadvantages. I'll sure be glad if I can convince my niece from Dallas to join my practice. Jessica specializes in business law, so she would have handled this, for instance."

"But if she works for you, won't you still have to worry about conflicts of interest?" Dax asked.

"Sure. For example, she couldn't take one side of a case and me another, since she'd be in my firm. But at least I won't have to play poker with my friends at night and maybe be forced to battle against them during the day."

"When does she get here to check things out?"

Ford sighed. "I expect her in the next day or two. And I can't tell you how glad I am. The sooner I have a little help around here, the better. I'm at the stage where I'd like to start taking things easier, and with the town booming, that isn't likely."

"Good news, bad news," Dax said. "Sort of like my relationship with Chloe."

"You can do something about that. It's in your power."

Dax nodded. "Yes, and I've been thinking that maybe the thing for me to do is put an offer on the table. I've been waiting for her to make the first offer, since she wanted to factor in the future growth of the town, but I see now that might not be the way to go."

"I couldn't agree more. It's way too speculative and I'm glad that at least one of you realizes that. Of course, that doesn't mean that compensation can't be made in some other way that would accomplish the same result."

"Yes, I suppose that's true," Dax said.

"Well, I think it's safe to say my client wants to deal. She sure as the devil didn't come all the way out here to taste the buffalo stew."

And then, a few hours after his conversation with Ford, Quentin Starr had come calling, adding even more pressure to an already touchy situation. Dax had been in his office, going over the numbers of his offer to Chloe, when Starr's lanky frame filled the doorway. He didn't need to consult old Alma Jones, who passed for the town seer, to know that Quentin wanted to talk to him about the Cowboy Club.

"I've been expecting to hear talk you've bought out Chloe's interest in the club," Quentin said after they'd dispensed with the niceties. "But the word around town is it hasn't happened. Don't mean to pry, but as you know, the lady did talk to me about selling the other night. Rather than ask her what's up, I thought the decent thing would be to ask you instead. Has the situation changed, or is that none of my business?"

"I appreciate your coming by to speak about it, Quentin," Dax told him. "The fact is, I'm about to put a firm offer on the table. I expect to have the sale wrapped up in a matter of days."

"Sounds like I was wise to give you a holler before sticking my nose in, then."

"Well, it's not my place to announce that her interest in the club is off the market, but I'm expecting that to be the case shortly."

"So it sounds like I should be looking for other places to put my money," Quentin said.

"That'd be my advice."

Dax had taken Quentin out and bought him a beer, then went back to work in earnest on putting together a firm offer for Chloe. Though he was sure the timing of Quentin Starr's visit was coincidental, it served as a reminder that he was skating on thin ice. Time was of the essence.

And looking at the clock, he saw it was getting on time to head over to see Ford. Dax gathered his papers. He'd outlined an offer. Ford could dot the i's and cross the t's. The sooner he and Chloe got this behind them, the sooner they could concentrate on their personal relationship.

He'd already planned a romantic evening. They were going to have dinner and then dance, as this was the night that they had a live band at the Cowboy Club. With any luck, they'd have struck their deal and this would be a celebration. He hoped so. They'd never danced together, and the notion of having her in his arms—in public, in front of the whole

damn town, or as many of them that showed up—
was appealing. Very appealing.

He asked himself why that was, and realized that
he was proud to be seen with Chloe. He was proud
of her, too. She had guts, the kind of guts it took to
start her own business and make it work, even
through the rough times. That took character. And
he could tell she genuinely cared about people. She'd
gone out of her way to be helpful to both Wanda and
Erica.

In the past, Dax had never given a fig what anyone
thought about the women he dated, probably because he hadn't cared enough about any of them to
wonder what his friends might think. But that wasn't
true now. He couldn't imagine anything he'd like
more than being with Chloe in the middle of the
dance floor of the Cowboy Club.

That made him smile. The last time they'd been on
the dance floor had been the night they'd met. Then
he had regarded her as an adversary, a problem.
Now everything had changed, though a part of him
still wasn't sure if that was for the better or not. Life
had gotten complicated. Maybe too complicated.

Once more, he thought about Quentin Starr. What
worried him most was how much he should tell
Chloe, if anything, about Starr's visit. What was the
honorable thing to do? Sure, he and Chloe were
sleeping together, but that didn't mean that he had to
tell her everything. Or did it?

Never before had he faced a situation like this.
True, he hadn't made a practice of sleeping with
women he did business with, but that wasn't the issue as much as his feelings. He respected Chloe and
wanted her to respect him. He cared about what she
thought. And he didn't want to hurt her.

Dax checked the pendulum clock on the wall

again, the one Cody had carefully wound every Monday morning as long as he'd lived. Dax sighed, getting to his feet. If Cody was there now, what would he advise? That was a hard one, Dax knew. Cody had treated him like a son, but Chloe was his niece. In all probability, the old man would've worried that one or both of them might be hurt.

What it boiled down to, he realized, was that for the first time in a long time he cared. There had been a lot of women in his life, but no one permanent. The idea of commitment had never held much appeal. He was thinking like a man who was afraid of losing something special…and he wasn't sure whether he liked that feeling or not.

CHLOE WAS LAYING OUT the black silk shantung dress she was going to wear for her date that night, when the phone rang. It was Ford Lewis.

"Chloe, I've just spent the past half hour with Dax Charboneau," he said. "He's presented an offer to buy your interest in the Cowboy Club."

She was surprised. "He gave *you* the offer?"

"Well, I think Dax felt it would be the most businesslike way to handle it. He said he'd rather dance with you and negotiate with me," Ford said, chuckling.

That came as a relief. She'd been anguishing about whether or not she should drop her demand for compensation for future economic growth. "Well, how does the offer look?" she asked nervously.

"It's generous, very generous in terms of price. Dax has set the gross value of the club at a million dollars. That includes the building, fixtures, personal property and goodwill."

"The appraised value was nine hundred thousand, wasn't it?"

"That's right. In exchange for terms, and because he wants to take into account that the town is on the verge of booming, he's offering you a hundred thousand over appraisal."

"So, what do I get, exactly?" she asked.

"Well, there's a two-hundred-and-fifty-thousand-dollar loan on the property which makes the equity in the business seven hundred and fifty thousand. Your half would be three hundred seventy-five thousand dollars. He's offering ten thousand cash and a ten-year note for the balance at ten percent interest. The income to you on the note would be four thousand eight hundred and twenty-five dollars per month."

Chloe sat back in her chair, pondering what she'd just heard. She'd been hoping to come away with a quarter of a million dollars. Dax was offering her substantially more, but mostly in the form of a note. The ten thousand would barely cover her expenses, but having nearly five thousand coming in each month wasn't bad.

"I'm not very knowledgeable about restaurants, Ford," she said, "but I do know carrying a large note on a business isn't a good idea."

"It all comes down to if the operator can generate sufficient cash flow to run the business and service the debt. According to the books, the income is there. The question is if you trust Dax to keep the ship afloat until you've been paid off."

"He has been running the Cowboy Club successfully for a long time," she said, "I guess that means something." Chloe pondered the situation. "What do you think, Ford?"

"I can't tell you whether to take the deal or not," he replied. "From a business and legal standpoint, I'd like you to get more cash up front, but on the other hand the purchase price is quite generous and he'd be paying real good interest. What Dax is doing, Chloe, is asking you to trust him and to give him time to pay you off."

"Well, it wasn't what I had in mind when I came," she said. "But five thousand coming in each month is not bad. It'll cover most of my own operating expenses. My banker will like it almost as much as cash."

"What do you want me to tell Dax, then?" Ford asked.

Chloe tried to think of the deal in cold, hard business terms, but it was difficult not to think of the man behind the offer. She sighed, feeling torn. This was the first offer she'd gotten, and if she waited, Quentin Starr or someone else might come to the bargaining table. On the other hand, he might not.

"We can always counteroffer," Ford said, interrupting her thoughts. "Maybe ask for more cash up front."

"I don't know if there's any point in haggling," she replied. "Another five or ten thousand won't make that much difference and Dax probably doesn't have it right now anyway. I wouldn't want him dipping into his operating reserves."

"Shall I tell him you accept, then?"

Chloe hesitated, picturing Dax's handsome, smiling face. It wasn't professional, she knew, but she also couldn't help thinking about their discussion about partners. From what Dax had said, he wanted to run the show, which she could certainly understand—heavens, she'd felt that way about her own business. And he *had* offered her more than the appraised value, considerably more. "Yes, tell him the Cowboy Club is entirely his."

Chloe hung up the phone, feeling a burden had

been lifted. Until now she hadn't realized how much this had been weighing on her. But even as one worry was solved, another reared its ugly head. What would happen now? Cutting a deal had been her excuse for staying in Red Rock—and being with Dax.

Chloe sat down on the bed, next to the black dress. Smoothing the fabric of the skirt, she thought about their plans for that evening. Dinner and dancing had seemed romantic when Dax mentioned it. Not that their relationship had been a big secret or anything, but this was sort of letting it all hang out, proclaiming to the town that they were interested in each other. She'd liked the idea of that. It lent significance to what they had together.

If she'd been smarter, she probably would have tried to view Dax as a summer romance—fun while it lasted, then adios with no regrets. But she didn't want to say goodbye. She'd connected with Dax, really connected, and she didn't want to give that up.

The hell of it was, it wasn't entirely her decision. Dax might be glad that things between them were winding down. Or, even if he was sad to see her go, it didn't mean that he'd want her to stick around indefinitely. Sighing, she realized that the best thing she could do would be to prepare herself for the end. That was the only option that made sense.

Her preoccupation with the issue culminated when Carlo called with some great news. "Chloe, we just got a fax from that princess in the royal family of Kuwait who gave us the two huge orders. Some cousins of hers will be in New York next week. She asks if you'll see them at their hotel. They love the princess's shoes and want to know what you can do for them."

"Carlo, that's fabulous!"

"Yes," he said. "I knew you'd be pleased. But will you be here to talk to them?"

"I've got some news of my own. I've wrapped up my deal here and I should be home in a few days."

"So, it went well?"

"Pretty well, yes."

"With all the orders you've been taking, I was afraid you'd be moving your business to Colorado for good," he joked.

Chloe wondered if, despite his kidding, he might not actually have been concerned. He and Donatella had worked for her for a long time, and Carlo had said that he planned on staying with her until he retired in a decade or so, at which time he wanted to move to Arizona or California or even New Mexico.

"Oh, by the way," Carlo said, "I finished the sandals for the lady in the restaurant and shipped them this morning. You should get them tomorrow."

"Great. How are the wedding shoes coming? I'd like to give those to Erica before I leave."

"You said to rush, so I should be finished with them before I leave tonight."

"That's wonderful, Carlo. Get them to me as quickly as you can."

"I will."

"Thanks for the call and the good news. Plan on seeing me in a few days."

"It'll be good to have you home," he said.

Chloe hung up, wishing she shared his enthusiasm for getting back to normal. It would be good to be in her studio again, but something she'd found in Red Rock would be missing—a man she cared about. Which reminded her, she had to get ready for an evening of dinner and dancing with Dax. It would be a challenge to get through it with a smile on her face and avoid any tears, but she'd met a lot of challenges in her time. Why should this be any different?

Chloe turned her thoughts to the little black dress she planned to wear. With its cap sleeves and slim skirt, it was a classic. But she still hadn't decided what shoes to wear. In the end she chose the silver shoes with their high heels and sexy straps—among her all-time favorites.

After bathing and doing her hair, she slipped on her dress, then the shoes. She took a final look in the mirror on the front of the old pine armoire that stood in the corner of the room. Turning first one way, then another to check out her outfit, she decided that she looked good. Oh, that one stubborn dark curl was hanging over her forehead, but that was nothing new.

Knowing it was time to get going, she grabbed her purse and left. Within minutes she had parked her car across the street from the Cowboy Club and was making her way inside. The first person she saw was Wanda.

"Lordy, if you don't look beautiful," the hostess said. "And you wore those silver shoes. I was hoping you would."

Chloe glanced down at her feet. "You don't think they're too much?" she asked.

"Can't have too much of a good thing, Chloe. Of course, before the night is over, every woman in the place will have turned pea green with envy, but that's the way it goes. Besides, it'll give them something new to talk about."

"Well, if you're sure…" She looked around the room and didn't see Dax. "Is he in his office?"

Wanda nodded.

"Then I'll head on back. By the way," she said,

"your sandals should be here tomorrow. Carlo is sending them to me by courier."

Wanda grinned and held out her foot. "The old dogs are ready, I can tell you that. If I had the shoes now, I might just go out on that dance floor myself. It's been a while, but I haven't forgotten how."

"Yes. You should. Even if you have to take off your shoes."

Wanda chuckled. "You know, I might do that. After all, my boss made the suggestion, so you can hardly fire me for it."

With that, Wanda turned to help a couple who had just come in, and Chloe headed for the back room. As she walked through the club, she could feel the eyes of everyone on her. She was still a curiosity, she knew, but no one had been unkind. In fact, most folks had gone out of their way to be friendly.

She saw Wiley Cooper at a table with a lovely brunette who had startling deep blue eyes. The woman was wearing a red dress that was obviously designer quality. And her haircut had "city" written all over it. Chloe figured she must be visiting.

Chloe gave Wiley a quick smile then turned to check out the people at the bar, thinking she might spot Ford. He had said he'd be by later on, and she knew he liked to sit at the bar, nursing the one drink he allowed himself as he watched everyone have a good time. Ford wasn't there, and neither was Heath. She expected that one or both of them would show up before the evening was over, though.

Continuing past the dance floor, she walked down the short hallway to Dax's office. The door was shut, so she knocked.

"Come on in," she heard him say.

Chloe, nervous despite herself, went in.

11

WHEN SHE CAME into the room, Dax felt his heart bump. Chloe looked so beautiful, so heart-wrenchingly adorable with that one fat curl hanging over her right eye, that he wanted to take her into his arms and kiss her senseless. Instead, he got up from his chair and gave her a soft kiss on the cheek. "You look beautiful."

"Thanks, I try to do my best." She smiled. "After all, I wouldn't want to let a former partner down…"

Dax nodded. "You could never let me down. And may I say that, as a *former* partner, I'm glad that we have something to celebrate. Not that a reason is necessary."

He took her hand and led the way back out to the restaurant to the table he'd reserved. It was the same one they had been in the first time he'd seen her. He wondered if Chloe would say anything about that. Probably. Women always noticed those things.

"Looks like the boss reserved the table closest to the dance floor for himself," Chloe said as she slipped into the booth.

Dax smiled to himself. "Nothing but the best. After all, it isn't every day I cut a deal to buy the Cowboy Club."

Wanda came up to the table then with a bottle of champagne. "I believe this is the one you told Ben to have ready," she said, putting the wine bucket on a stand next to the booth. "Do you want your hors d'oeuvres now or later?"

He turned to Chloe. "Are you hungry?"

"I can wait if you can."

"Why not give us a while to enjoy the champagne?" Dax said.

With that, Wanda left. Dax stood, took the bottle from the bucket and opened it. Then he filled two glasses, handing one to Chloe. "Here's to the most beautiful partner I ever had," he said, clinking his glass to hers.

He saw the rose stain her cheeks as she took a quick sip of wine. He wondered if he'd embarrassed her. He didn't see how. It wasn't as if they were strangers, like the first time they'd been at this table. Yet Chloe seemed different tonight. Almost as if she was holding back.

"Are you okay?" he said, setting down his glass as he sat next to her once more.

"I'm fine. A little tired, maybe. I had a good conversation with Carlo. Business is booming. I may get substantial orders from relatives of a Kuwaiti princess client. The women will be in New York next week and I'm going to meet with them."

Dax heard the words, and he also heard the message behind them. He'd known she'd have to leave sooner or later, but listening to her say the words made it seem more immediate…and real.

"You're planning on leaving soon, then?"

She nodded. "Yes. I have a few loose ends to tie up and then I'm off."

"What sort of loose ends?"

"Well, I've got to sign the contract for one thing. And deliver Wanda her shoes. Carlo shipped them today and they should be here in the morning. And

Erica's wedding shoes should be here the day after that."

"I see."

He watched her face carefully, but for once she wasn't betraying her thoughts. He wasn't sure what that meant. She had to feel something, didn't she? But if so, he didn't have the slightest idea what. Dax took another sip of champagne, watching her. She was being pleasant but distant. Not at all the way she'd been the last few days. Why?

He reached over and took her hand. It was cool, silky. He stared at her fingers and recalled the feel of them on his skin. Her touch had put him on fire, made him want to make love to her until he barely had the strength to move—and they'd done just that several nights running. So why did she seem different tonight? Hell, she was the same woman, wasn't she?

"You're not drinking your champagne," he said.

Chloe immediately picked up her glass. "Sorry. I guess my mind is on business. I've been trying to decide whether I should have a variety of designs ready when I meet the ladies from Kuwait, or wait until I talk to them and find out what they have in mind."

Dax gave her a confident smile. It nearly killed him. What he wanted to do was grit his teeth, yell, grab her by the shoulders and shake her...anything to make her react. For the life of him, he couldn't figure out what was wrong. Everything suddenly seemed backward, inside out.

Why?

Chloe had come to Red Rock to make a deal. Well, they'd done it. And despite the fact that he'd be paying her more than the business was worth, she didn't seem happy. Hell, she seemed more as if she was ready to go to a funeral than a celebration. Then he dared think what he'd secretly been hoping—she was sad about leaving and was putting up a brave front. The notion made his heart soar, though reason told him there was no guarantee that was what was behind her change of mood.

He was watching her sip champagne and trying to figure out how to bridge the distance separating them when Wanda brought over a huge plate of hors d'oeuvres—snake bites and armadillo eggs. He picked up one of the pieces of barbecued snake and offered it to Chloe. She shook her head.

"I think I'll pass. I know you have a special dinner planned, and if I want to dance, I can't eat everything in sight."

Dax popped the morsel into his own mouth and chewed, all the while trying to tell himself that her refusal was perfectly logical. But there was intent behind it, too. He'd bet good money on it. Another message.

"Oh, look," Chloe said, motioning toward the bar. "Ford is here. Do you think we ought to invite him over? After all, he's drawing up the papers for the deal."

Dax had no particular desire to share her, but he had to play the good soldier. "Good idea," he said with as much enthusiasm as he could muster. "I'll go ask him to join us." With that, he slid out of the booth and headed for the bar.

As he strode across the still-empty dance floor, Dax rubbed his chin. Damn. This wasn't working out the way he'd planned. He'd wanted a nice romantic evening. He'd wanted to show Chloe off, celebrate that they were an item. And sure, celebrate the sale of the club, too. But he'd planned this evening before he'd even known he would make Chloe a firm offer. The business part was secondary. Or had been. Now he was beginning to wonder if either celebration would get off the ground.

Ford was looking in the big gilt mirror over the bar, watching him approach as he sipped his bourbon and branch. Dax grinned, giving him a wink.

"Have you come here to rejoice in the prospect of your upcoming legal fees for preparing the Cowboy Club contract?"

Ford Lewis chuckled. "No, more like I'm celebrating the fact that my life is about to get a little easier. At least, I hope it is." With that, he paused dramatically.

Dax knew that Ford had something he wanted to say and he didn't want to deny his old friend the opportunity to spin the tale out slowly. "And what, pray tell, has changed since I saw you this afternoon, if you don't mind my asking?"

Ford nodded toward where Wiley was sitting with a good-looking brunette. She must have come in while Dax was in his office because he'd never seen her before. She was wearing a red dress and looked rather sophisticated, not unlike Chloe in that sense.

"My niece, Jessica, got into town about two hours ago. Wiley was in my office at the time, dropping off a book he'd promised to loan me, when she arrived."

"And our favorite newspaperman is dining with her already?"

Ford nodded.

Dax whistled. "Fast work. Didn't know Wiley had it in him."

Ford chuckled. "Just shows what a guy can do once he doesn't have you around for competition." He winked at Dax as he took another sip. "You seem to be well taken care of."

"Speaking of which, Chloe and I would like you to

join us. We're celebrating the deal. And since you helped make it possible…"

Ford seemed to ponder that, taking a sip of his drink before he answered. "I guess that means you want me to come over long enough to be friendly, have a snake bite or two then make myself scarce."

Dax grinned. "If it wouldn't be too much trouble. Long enough to be sociable."

"But not too long, right?" Ford got off the bar stool. "It's the least I can do, I suppose."

"I didn't mean to hurt your feelings, Ford."

"Think nothing of it. I've already been stood up once today…when Jessica decided to dine with Wiley. Believe me, I'm glad for any scrap of society I'm offered. Besides, it will do my reputation good to have it look like someone wants my company."

As they started back to the table, Dax wondered if having another person around would change Chloe's mood. In a way, he hoped it would lighten things. But in another way, he was afraid what that might mean. Was she tentative because of something he'd done or failed to do, or was it something else? He didn't know, but he was determined to find out which it was before the night ended.

CHLOE WATCHED as Ford and Dax made their way across the dance floor. She pasted a happy smile on her face and stood to greet Ford, holding out her hand. "I'm so glad you're joining us. I looked for you when I came in, but you weren't at the bar."

"Just got here," Ford said, shaking her hand. He slid into the booth next to her, setting his drink down in front of him.

Dax slid in across from her. "Will you be able to join us for dinner?" she asked.

Ford harrumphed. "Nope. I just stopped by for a

snake bite or two…and to tell you I'll have those contracts ready by noon tomorrow, as promised. In fact, my niece just blew into town, so I'll have her look them over, as well. Jessica specializes in business law."

"Oh?"

"Yep. She's a widow, from Dallas. Lost her husband and her baby girl in a terrible accident. She's here to talk about joining my practice." Ford popped a snake bite into his mouth. "Just in time, too. If I want to run for mayor again, I'll need a helping hand at the office."

"Heavens, we wouldn't want a little thing like the law to get in the way of a political career, now, would we?" She winked at Dax.

"Lord, no," Dax chimed in. "Ford here has his priorities straight. Poker on Thursday nights, enough law to keep the wolf from the door, and the rest of the time he can kiss babies and beautiful girls."

Ford had a slight smile on his lips as he took a sip of his bourbon and branch. "Now, you young folks can make fun if you want, but being mayor around here is damn near a full-time job. Seems like there's something happening all the time…which is why we're attracting people like Quentin Starr and my niece, Jessica."

"Speaking of which," Dax said as he swallowed an armadillo egg, "you'll have to introduce us to her." He turned to Chloe. "She's the brunette sitting with Wiley. I don't know if you noticed her when you came in."

"I did. She's lovely." Chloe picked up her glass and took a sip, thankful that Ford had joined them. It made talking a little easier.

"Well," Ford said, draining the last of his bourbon. "I best be going. I planned on having my one drink and then returning to the office for a spell. I want to have some files pulled for Jessica to look over in the morning. So, if you'll excuse me…"

"Sure you can't stay?" Chloe asked.

The lawyer shook his head. "Nope. See you in the morning, Chloe. Bye, Dax."

Chloe watched as he headed off, stopping a time or two to say hello to someone. Then she turned to Dax. "What's next on the menu?"

"Ben has gotten a few golden trout from a friend. Not enough to put on the menu for tonight, but enough to make a special dinner for us. If you've never had any, you're in for a real treat."

"Good," Chloe said. "I could use a treat. After all, this will be one of my last meals in Red Rock."

She saw the pained expression on Dax's face as he filled her glass then topped off his own.

"So," he said, "are you looking forward to dancing?"

She looked into his eyes before she answered. For the first time she saw a trace of doubt in them. "Well, I have my dancing shoes on," she said in answer to his question. "But don't expect too much. It's been an age since I've danced, and never to western tunes."

"Just follow my lead, Chloe, and you'll be fine."

His voice as he spoke was low and sexy—like when they were in bed. Chloe was sure there was a hidden message in the "follow my lead" phrase. But again, she did not know what.

Well, she thought, maybe Dax was right. Maybe she should just follow his lead, try to enjoy herself and not worry too much about tomorrow. It seemed to work for him. With luck, it might be the best way for her to end her time in Red Rock as gracefully as possible.

IF DAX HAD BEEN ABLE to script the remainder of the evening, he wasn't sure how he'd have wanted things to go, other than that he hoped Chloe would enjoy being with him as much as he enjoyed being with her.

Thank God, she seemed more relaxed now than she had at first. But he wasn't willing to simply take the manna handed him and go merrily on his way. He wanted to understand *why* she'd been tentative earlier. Somehow, knowing the reason mattered. In fact, for the first time ever so far as he could recall, a woman's feelings and needs were more important to him than his own.

On the plus side, the dancing had gone well. Despite what Chloe had said, when he took her in his arms she followed his lead as if they'd been partners for years. And when they slow danced, she'd moved real close to him and sighed softly. He inhaled the fresh scent of her hair and knew that this moment was exactly what he'd been looking forward to. Then Wiley had shown up out of nowhere and ruined everything by cutting in on him.

Dax pasted a tight smile on his face, and they changed partners. Jessica Kilmer, Ford's niece, was very pretty in a refined, sophisticated way. She had deep blue eyes and shoulder-length dark hair, and she looked to be in her early thirties. Their dance had been pleasant. He'd tried to be friendly, keep up his end of the conversation, but all the while they danced he was maneuvering around the floor so that he could keep an eye on Chloe. She was laughing at something Wiley had said, and gave every appearance of being happy and relaxed.

The music stopped and, seeing that Wiley had taken Chloe back to their table, Dax escorted Jessica there, as well. After introducing the women, Wiley suggested they have a drink together. But first, Jessica insisted she simply had to get a better look at Chloe's silver shoes. So while Dax and Wiley slid into the booth, Chloe lifted her foot to the seat of the banquette so that Jessica could check them out.

"They're even more gorgeous than I thought," Jessica said. "I noticed them when you came in, and also on the dance floor. Do you mind telling me where you got them?"

Chloe smiled as she put her foot back on the floor. "I made them. I design and make custom shoes for a living."

"Here in Red Rock?" Jessica asked. "I thought you could only get shoes like yours in New York, London or Paris."

"Well, you're partly right," Chloe said. "I am from New York, but I've already designed shoes for several of Red Rock's fairest, so you don't have to live there to buy my wares."

Before the women had a chance to sit down, John and Kate MacInnes came up to their booth. Dax stood to greet them. Then, after introducing the couple to Jessica and Chloe, he turned to John and said, "Well, what brings the two of you out tonight?"

"We're celebrating," John said, suddenly puffing out his chest all proud-like. "Kate here has gotten herself pregnant again."

"Not without a little help from you, dear," the blonde said, laughing.

Dax slapped John on the back and reached over to kiss Kate's cheek. "The drinks are on the house, then. But I take it no alcohol for you…"

Kate nodded. "Not for the duration." She turned to Chloe. "Do you mind if I have a closer look at your shoes, too? I spotted them on the dance floor and told

John that they were the sexiest things I'd ever seen. I just had to come over and get a better look."

"Sure," Chloe said, laughing as she put her foot back up on the seat of the banquette.

While the women got into the whole shoe-discussion thing again, Dax called Wanda over and ordered drinks for everyone. They also brought a couple more chairs so that John and Kate could join them. When Wanda left, everyone finally sat down.

Kate spoke first. "John, you have to get me a pair of dancing shoes like those."

He rolled his eyes and turned to Dax and Wiley. "She knows I can't say no to her when she's pregnant. In fact, she did so well on our first two that I'm amazed we don't have ten children by now."

Kate slapped his wrist playfully. "It's the least you can do. After all, look what I'll be going through. Why, before this is over I'll be so fat I won't want to look in the mirror. But with sexy shoes like Chloe's, at least one part of me will still look good."

"A part you won't be able to see by the eighth month," John teased.

Chloe and Jessica laughed as Kate gave her husband a dirty look. "Just get me those shoes. I love them."

John turned to Chloe. "Can you make her a pair? I don't care what they cost, so long as she's happy."

"Words I love to hear," Chloe said.

"Me, too," Kate chimed in.

"I'm not going to touch this one." Jessica laughed. "Besides, I think the two of you are doing all right without my help."

The drinks came shortly after that, and everyone seemed to be having a good time. But even with the talk about babies and new law practices, all Dax could think about was what Kate had said about

Chloe's shoes being sexy. Kate was right. In fact, everything about Chloe was sexy—not overtly, maybe, but in a way that called to him.

He liked the way she blushed every time she was flustered, and the way that one fat curl tended to fall over her forehead. And when they made love, he liked the sound of the little cries of pleasure she made just before she climaxed.

Of course, nice as all that was, it wouldn't be enough, not if he didn't like the way her mind worked. Like him, she marched to a different drummer. Dax watched her talking to John MacInnes about his ranch. Chloe might be from New York, but she was a people person and she seemed to find a way to fit in no matter where she was. And she was so beautiful as she sat there talking, sipping wine, her black dress so quietly elegant even if those silver shoes of hers did scream, "Look at me, I'm sexy!"

Lord knew, he wanted to do a hell of a lot more than look. In fact, if he had his way, right now he'd be at Cody's, taking off that perfect little black dress, and the lacy black bra and bikini panties that he was sure she had on under it. But he wanted her to leave on the silver shoes when he made love with her. They'd never done that, and he wanted this to be a night to remember.

IT WAS ALMOST MIDNIGHT, and Chloe was slow dancing with Dax. Sometime during the last hour she'd decided to give in to her feelings. She was falling in love with Dax, whether he wanted that kind of relationship or not. And she wanted to be with him. As he held her close in his arms, Chloe breathed in his scent. Why was it that no other man had smelled like that—like the wind on a summer evening?

The music stopped and she looked into Dax's eyes.

They were full of passion and promise. She'd seen that look before. But how many times would she see it again?

Then Dax asked the question she'd been waiting for all evening. Would she spend the night with him?

Though she'd been expecting to hear the words, her heart had missed a beat. But she'd whispered in his ear, "Of course. I'd love to be with you one more time."

Dax pulled back to better see her expression. "What do you mean, one more time?"

She put her head on his shoulder so he couldn't see her face. "Tomorrow I'll be packing. Besides, I'll need to get a good rest before the drive back to Denver."

Dax hadn't questioned her further. She'd watched closely to see if he seemed rattled by her statement, but he didn't appear to be. Which told her all she needed to know. Now all she had to do was think of this as a one-time chance to really let down her hair with no thought of tomorrow. God knew, the consequences would come soon enough. They always did.

They drove to Cody's house in the Bronco. When they got to the front door, Chloe handed him the key. Dax opened the door and ushered her in. She could feel the tension in the air. He wanted her as much as she wanted him. Yet there was something different about tonight. Their last night.

"Can I get you something to drink?" she asked simply.

He shook his head. "I'm fine. The only thing I want is you."

She took a deep breath when he said those words, moved by the low growl of his voice. She *did* want him. Maybe too much. And though it would be hard making love while knowing that this would be the last time, Chloe knew she didn't have it in her to turn him away. Even if she never saw Dax again, there was no way she could find it in her heart to regret these days in Red Rock. They were too special. Dax was too special.

He walked up to her and put his arms around her waist. She gazed into his eyes and he kissed her forehead where a curl fell over her eye. Then he said, "But I have a special request. Would you leave your shoes on?"

Chloe leaned back to look at him. There was a definite gleam in his eye…a gleam she liked. "I think that can be arranged," she replied.

She kissed him then, with a passion and a need she'd never felt before. It was strong and poignant, and somewhere deep in her soul something stirred. Yet even as she realized that, Chloe closed her eyes and felt the world start to slip away. There were no more fears, no thoughts of tomorrow. There was only Dax.

She felt his arms tighten around her waist. She ran her fingers through the thick hair at the back of his neck. And through it all, they kissed. Finally, breathless, Chloe pulled away. She turned her back to him and swept her hair up off her neck. "I'll need help with my zipper."

Dax didn't say a word as he slowly unzipped her dress, kissing the back of her neck when he was finished. She shivered. Then, turning once more to give him a quick smile, she headed for the bedroom.

She had stepped out of the dress and was hanging it in the closet when Dax came into the room. This was the moment she'd been waiting for—when he'd discover that she was wearing silver lace lingerie.

"My, oh my," he said, leaning against the doorjamb. "I've spent the evening picturing you in black lace. If I'd known you were wearing silver, to match your shoes, and a silver garter belt, I'd have pulled you into the back room and made love to you on the poker table."

She felt a stab of something in her gut—regret, maybe, that she'd never hear these words again. But this wasn't a time for regrets. It was go-for-broke night. "I take it that means you approve?"

For an answer he took a couple of quick strides over to her so he could gather her into his arms. He gave her a hard kiss, then stepped back to regard her again. "As long as I live, I want to remember the way you look right now," he murmured.

The first thought that rolled through Chloe's mind was that would be a long time, decades and decades. Would he remember her that long? Was he doing the same thing she was trying to do—storing up memories?

She couldn't ask, so she put her arms around his neck. And when he kissed her she gave herself up to it completely.

It seemed to her as if every kiss she'd ever gotten, every sexual experience she'd ever had, had led her to this moment and this man. Being with Dax was what she'd been born for.

Within minutes Dax had her panting. He stripped off her bra and panties. And when she was left standing there in only her silver lace garter belt, hose and shoes, he knelt before her and pressed his face into her mound. His breath was warm, and when he blew on her, and traced her feminine lips with his index finger, she shivered. Chloe put her hands on his shoulders to steady herself. Dax pleasured her then, kissing and touching her until she was shaking with desire. He pulled away at length, and pressed his hand against her until she got control.

When her breathing slowed, Dax stood and undressed. Chloe watched him, committing to memory the breadth of his shoulders and the way he looked right into her eyes when he stripped, as if it was important to him to see her reaction. Then he led her to the bed. She knew then that if she lived a thousand years she'd never forget the feel of him when he first entered her, filling her so exquisitely and completely.

They made love with her legs wrapped around his waist. And when it was over, and he collapsed onto her, spent, it was several minutes before either of them spoke. "I think Kate was right," Dax whispered. "Those shoes are sexy, almost as irresistible as you."

Chloe played with the hair at the nape of his neck. "You think it was the shoes, do you?"

"If so, I predict that the MacInneses will be having a fourth in another year or so."

She didn't reply, just absently continued caressing the back of his neck. He rolled off her, encircling her with his arms, one of his legs over hers. In only a minute or so, she could tell he was asleep.

Chloe sighed. She was tired, but not sleepy. In a little while, Dax would probably wake up and they'd make love again. Just one or two more times would he be in her. One or two more times she'd be a part of him. One or two more times she'd feel complete—the woman she was meant to be.

She sighed, knowing she couldn't have resisted this no matter how high the price was. Yet despite her resolve, a part of her was already starting to regret that life was so unfair. Why couldn't Dax have been a Wall Street broker or a marketing executive? But then, he might not have been Dax—at least, not the Dax who'd just made love with her.

No, Dax Charboneau belonged to the West and to

Red Rock as surely as she belonged in New York City. She'd been a fish out of water from the moment she'd left home. After all, she'd been born and bred back East. She understood the mentality, the lifestyle. Red Rock was a vacation from that reality. And all vacations had to come to an end. Now it was almost time for this one to be over. She would return to her life, her work, her friends. But in her heart of hearts, she knew she'd never be able to forget Red Rock…or Dax. She'd just have to be content to carry a piece of them in her heart forever.

12

DAX AWOKE at dawn. He quietly slipped out of bed and dressed, careful not to make any noise. Chloe was finally sleeping. They had made love twice more during the night. He'd felt an urgency that left him wondering if he could ever get enough of her. They'd finished in the early hours of the morning.

Even so, he'd awakened once to hear her in the other room, pacing. He'd thought about getting up and asking what was wrong, but he had a feeling she wouldn't tell him. Chloe was working something out in her mind, and he owed it to her to give her space. At least, that's how he saw it.

Dax went into the kitchen and got the coffeepot ready so all she'd have to do when she woke up was plug it in. Cody's pot was old-fashioned and temperamental, and Chloe always had a hard time dealing with it. This was something he could do for her.

When he finished with the coffee, he wrote her a note and left it on the kitchen table. He'd see her later, either at the club or at Ford's to sign the contract. Meanwhile, he hoped she'd be able to get some rest.

Dax quietly stole out of the house, carefully locking the front door after him. Of course, there was no crime to speak of in Red Rock, but he wanted her to be safe all the same. No point in taking chances.

Dax climbed into his Bronco parked at the curb, right behind Chloe's rental car. He was glad it was still early because he had to drive clear out to his house to get cleaned up and dressed before heading to his office at the Cowboy Club.

As he drove, he wondered again about Chloe's mood. She'd been real quiet after they made love the second time. He'd taken off her shoes and kissed her from her feet all the way to the top of her head. There had been a desperation to their lovemaking that time, and afterward she'd softly cried.

He'd asked her what was wrong, but all she'd said was, "Nothing. I just get this way sometimes."

Dax didn't believe her. There was something else, he'd bet on it. But he didn't want to drag it out of her against her will, so instead he'd held her close, figuring that she was probably as upset as he was about her leaving. But what could they do? She wasn't about to pull up stakes and move to Colorado. And it had taken him years to find a home, a place where he truly fit in and felt like a part of the community. Besides, even if he did ask her to stay, what could he offer that could compete with the bright lights of New York City?

Dax turned onto the main highway out of town. Then he put a CD in the machine and listened to the jazz recording that he and Chloe liked best.

The real problem, he decided, was that they didn't have good choices. In the back of his mind, he'd known that it was unrealistic to expect her to hang around indefinitely. Yet that hadn't really hit him until she'd told him that she'd be willing to make love with him *one more time.* That had given him a jolt. Oh, he'd been able to put his feelings on the back burner for a while, but like it or not, reality was starting to sink in—a reality he didn't like.

The bottom line was, Chloe's playtime in Red Rock had come to an end. There was no longer a good reason for her to stick around. At least, *he'd* given her no good reason. Lord, that was what it had come to, he suddenly realized. Commitment.

His dilemma was becoming clearer by the moment. Were his feelings strong enough to talk in terms of a long-term relationship, a committed one? Of course, there was no way to be certain that she'd be interested in that, even if he were. But Dax knew that the discussion had to begin somewhere. The question was, how far was he willing to go to get her to stay?

He reached his house, and by the time he'd showered, dressed and made breakfast, it was nearly seven. Dax looked at the piece of toast with strawberry jelly smeared over it. He'd made wheat toast and coffee for himself thousands and thousands of times, but this morning it seemed different somehow. Empty. Maybe because the memory of making toast for Chloe just a couple of days ago was still fresh in his mind.

Dax took a swig of coffee and sighed. He and Chloe had spent only a handful of nights together, yet here he was, pining over the prospect of losing her. Could she really mean that much to him? So quickly?

As he sat there, fretting about his sanity, he got a call from Heath Barnett.

"Just got off the phone with Morgan Prescott, old buddy," Heath said excitedly. "Today's the day. Morgan says cattle futures have hit bottom and he thinks it's time to buy in."

Dax blinked as if he'd fallen into a time warp. The last thing on his mind was business, which should have told him something right there. "That money's been tucked away so long, it feels like it's already been spent," he finally said.

"Well, it has, Dax, it has. We've just been waiting for the right moment."

As the news sank in, Dax couldn't help feeling a surge of excitement. The three of them stood to make a pile of dough, for no other reason than that they were willing to take a chance. When you stopped to think about it, the markets were only another form of gambling, not unlike a game of poker. The only difference was trading investments instead of chips had a certain cachet, the color of respectability. But it was still gambling.

Dax remembered the day Heath had first brought Prescott to the Cowboy Club. Like most folks, Dax had been impressed. Prescott was one of the wealthiest men in the state. Seemed as if he owned damn near as much of Denver as Dax owned of Red Rock. Yet Prescott was a regular guy, a onetime cowpoke who'd made it big in ranching and took his nose for making money to other endeavors like real estate development and high-tech investments.

Morgan had been a good friend of Heath's father and the two had made money in the past betting futures. When Heath's dad died, Prescott had promised him he'd cut his son in on the next big opportunity to come along. Heath hadn't had the two hundred thousand necessary to buy in, so, with Prescott's permission, he'd brought Dax in with him, each of them pledging a hundred thousand.

"I hope this pays off," Dax told him.

"If Prescott's to be believed, we could triple our money in sixty to ninety days."

"Or lose two-thirds of it," Dax said.

"Since when have you been afraid to cut the cards?" Heath asked.

"Gambling's not the problem. It's what I had to

give up to be at the table. I came real close to not being able to make a deal for the Cowboy Club."

"Well, you'll be glad you kept hold of your capital," Heath assured him. "Morgan will be calling me back, but he said we'll probably have to wire our share to a brokerage account. I'll let you know. You going to be at the club, Dax?"

"Should be there most of the day."

"I'll drop by later, then," Heath said. "See ya."

Dax hung up the phone with a sigh. Normally a call like that would have made his day. He liked action, the wheeling and dealing. But this business with Chloe had gotten him down. And the worst part of it was, he still wasn't sure what to do about it.

CHLOE WAS STANDING at the living-room window, wistfully thinking about her wonderful night of lovemaking with Dax, when she noticed a UPS truck pull up in front of the house. Wanda's sandals had arrived. She went outside and met the deliveryman on the walkway. Taking the package from the driver, she saw that it was from Carlo, all right. She was glad. One less loose end to tie up.

Chloe checked the time. The night before, Ford had said he'd have her agreement with Dax ready to sign by noon. She'd go by his office and sign all the documents then. Another loose end would be tied up.

That was the way she'd tried to look at the world ever since she'd gotten up to find that Dax had already left. The dent in the pillow where his head had been said it all as far as she was concerned. She'd read his note. Fixing the coffeepot before he left had been real thoughtful. She'd tried hard to look at it as a final parting gesture—the act of a gentleman who looked out for her to the end.

But when Dax had gotten up to a new day, it was back to business as usual. For her, it was time to pay the piper. No more kidding herself. No more "last time to make love." This was it. The only unknown was how successful she'd be at not looking back on this time with regret.

So far, she wasn't doing too well. When she'd seen that Dax had readied the coffeepot, she'd thought of the mornings he had also made her toast and they had shared breakfast right along with their plans for the coming day. She sighed. Then she pulled herself together. With or without Dax, she had a life to live and a business to run. Feeling sorry for herself wouldn't change that.

Instead, she focused on the tasks ahead of her. She'd made her plane reservations. Packing wouldn't take long. She still had to make sure Erica got her wedding shoes, and she needed to measure Kate Mac-Innes's foot.

Chloe felt a wave of sadness at the thought of her silver shoes. After last night, making love to Dax with her shoes and garter belt on, there was no way she could ever see a pair of silver shoes again without remembering. She'd have to make herself scarce when Carlo was making the ones for Kate. And Chloe knew that she'd never, ever, wear her own silver slippers again. It would be too painful.

Chloe took the box of shoes for Wanda and went to the kitchen, where she got some scissors to cut the cord and open the package. She examined the sandals carefully. Carlo had done his usual fabulous job. Wanda would be thrilled, she was sure. Chloe placed the shoes in their individual cloth bags and was putting them back in the box when the phone rang. It was Mrs. Russo, her landlady in New York.

"Sorry to bother you on vacation," the woman began, "but something's come up. It's important, so Carlo gave me your number."

Chloe felt a well of trepidation. "What is it, Mrs. Russo?"

"I promised if I ever wanted to sell the loft, I'd give you a first right of refusal," she said. "Well, my late husband's cousin, Emile, came into a big inheritance and he's buying lots of real estate. He's already bought that little building of mine on the Upper East Side and he wants the loft, too."

Chloe's heart felt as if it rose right into her throat. "You're selling my loft?"

"Yes, I've been thinking of selling out for a couple of years now. Emile came along just at the right time. But I promised you first chance, so that's why I'm calling."

"What exactly do I have to do?" Chloe asked.

"Match Emile's price and terms. He'll pay two hundred and eighty thousand. All cash. Close in ten days."

"All cash in ten days? Mrs. Russo, I couldn't come up with that kind of money so quickly. I'd need a bank loan and more time."

"Carlo said you've sold a business in Colorado. Can't you use that money?"

"Yes, but I'm not getting cash. It's almost all in a note."

"Can't you change your deal or borrow against the note?"

"Mrs. Russo, I was lucky to get the deal I've got. I sold for a good price, but the money's going to be tied up for several years."

"I'm sorry, but I can't wait, not when I've got a buyer ready to write a check now."

"What are Emile's plans? Will he allow me to continue to rent the loft?"

"I can't speak for him," Mrs. Russo replied, "but I think he wants it for his daughter. She's a painter and wants a studio with good light."

"I can't lose the loft, Mrs. Russo. Not now. This couldn't come at a worse time."

"I'm really sorry, Chloe, but I'm not legally obligated to let you match Emile's offer. The only reason I'm doing it is because I promised. I want you to know, though, that I've sent legal notice for you to vacate the premises in case that becomes necessary."

Chloe swallowed hard. "Couldn't you take a note for part of the purchase price?" she asked, her desperation rising. "I'll pay you a higher price for the privilege."

The woman thought as Chloe agonized. Rents in New York were out of sight and she'd had a wonderful deal, considering the location. Mrs. Russo cleared her throat.

"If you come up with a hundred thousand down, I'll sell the loft for three hundred thousand. But it's got to be in ten days."

Chloe wondered how she could come up with a hundred thousand dollars so fast. Maybe somebody would give her cash for Dax's note on the Cowboy Club, but it would be at a huge discount and she'd lose lots of money. Her best bet would be to restructure her deal with Dax, but she'd already agreed to his offer.

"Mrs. Russo," Chloe said, "will you give me a couple of days? I should be back in New York day after tomorrow. I'll have an answer for you then."

The woman reluctantly agreed, and Chloe hung up. Only minutes ago she'd been worried about leaving Red Rock and Dax. Now she was in jeopardy of being thrown into the street along with her entire business. How things could have gone from bad to worse so fast, she had no idea. But this was a disaster, an absolute disaster.

DAX LEFT HIS OFFICE and went out into the bar to see how the lunch crowd was shaping up. It had been a morning of mixed emotions. It felt great to know that the Cowboy Club was now his—as soon as Chloe signed the deal, that is. Dax had fulfilled his end of the bargain by dropping off a check at Ford's office first thing that morning.

Almost as good, his long-awaited cattle futures deal was coming through. Things were really coming together. Yet, at the same time, he was on the verge of losing Chloe. Dax felt as if he was winning the battle, but losing the war.

Hearing a giggle from the dance floor, Dax turned to see Wanda doing pirouettes across the dark space. Then he saw Chloe, sitting on a banquette, watching her. Dax made his way to where Wanda was prancing around.

"How do you like my new shoes, boss?" Wanda said, seeing him coming.

He glanced down at her feet. "Hey, they look terrific."

"I can't believe how good they feel. My tootsies are in heaven!"

Dax looked over at Chloe, who was beaming with pride. "Another happy customer, it seems," he said.

"Wanda has a few foot problems. She had nowhere to go but up."

"I'm a new woman," Wanda said. "But duty calls. If you'll excuse me, I'll tend to our customers."

"Good idea, if you value your paycheck," Dax called after her with a laugh. Then he turned to Chloe. "They say the secret to a successful business is happy customers. I'd say you're at the top rung of the shoe business."

The faint smile on her lips faded. "I wish that's all there was to it."

He reached out and touched her cheek. "What's the matter? You don't look too chipper for a woman who just sold a nine-hundred-thousand-dollar business for a million bucks."

"Dax," she said, her expression turning sober. "I came to see you before going to sign the papers. I've...well, I've got a problem. And I thought we could talk about it."

He felt a clutch of uncertainty. God, she wasn't having second thoughts, was she? "What's the problem? You aren't going to try to get me to add another hundred grand to the purchase price, are you?"

"No, nothing like that. You were incredibly generous as it was," she said, her eyes glistening with tears. "But I'm in a fix. I'll put it to you straight. I got a call from New York this morning and it looks like I could be out on the street, with no place to go, in as little as a month."

"What happened?"

She explained the gist of Mrs. Russo's call. Dax listened gravely, knowing she wanted help in solving her problem.

"What would you like me to do?" he asked.

"I know we've made a deal," she replied, "but when I agreed to take only ten thousand up front, I had no idea this was going to happen. I desperately need a hundred thousand in cash to buy my loft. I talked to my accountant before coming here. Angela thinks I'll be able to cover the expense of the loan and service the debt if you're willing to restructure our deal."

"You're saying you want more cash."

"Yes, but I'm willing to lower the purchase price in return for more money up front. I'll drop the price to the appraised value."

"That's a hundred thousand less, but half of that's already mine," he replied. "I'd only save fifty thousand."

"It's not enough, in other words."

"I'm not trying to play hardball, Chloe. But whatever we do has to make economic sense."

She took a deep breath. "Okay, how would you feel if I lowered the price by a hundred and fifty thousand. That's seventy-five less you'll have to pay, if you can give me a hundred thousand cash up front."

Dax sighed. "I'd do it in a minute, if I could. But I don't have that kind of cash. Everything is already committed. I've been saying that all along. It wasn't a bargaining ploy."

"There's no way you can put your hands on the extra cash?"

Dax shook his head. "If I could, I would, Chloe." Tears welled from her eyes and he felt terrible. "Won't your bank advance you the money?" he said. "You've got a substantial asset in my note on the Cowboy Club."

"I asked Angela about that, and she's not optimistic, especially since they don't know you in New York. Besides, I've only got ten days. The one way I can see to salvage this is by getting extra cash from you."

Dax lowered his eyes. He thought of Quentin Starr and his pocketful of cash. If Starr had cut a deal with Chloe, she wouldn't be in this fix. Dax also thought of the nice fat check he'd write for the cattle deal. But he'd given Heath and Morgan his word—he was committed.

Now Chloe was paying the price for both of those deals, which isn't what he'd intended at all. Dammit, it hurt seeing her suffer.

"Are you sure you can't negotiate a lease with the new owner of the loft?"

"Yes. Mrs. Russo went so far as to give me notice to vacate, that's how sure she is."

"Your loft can't be the only suitable space in New York for a shoe design business," he said. "Have you checked your other options?"

"There are other places, of course. I can always find a warehouse-type facility in the Bronx or Brooklyn, but the setup I've got is in the heart of Manhattan, and the price is reasonable considering the location. This is the perfect opportunity for me, Dax." Her look turned beseeching. "Would it matter if I lowered the price of my half of the Cowboy Club to two hundred and fifty thousand?"

It was getting to the point where she was practically giving it away, which only made matters worse. "It's not a question of price, Chloe. It's liquidity. All my money is tied up."

She nodded, lowering her head. "I know," she said. "I just don't know what to do."

The knot in Dax's stomach felt like a rock. "If I beg and plead with my banker, I might be able to squeeze twenty or twenty-five thousand out of him," he said.

"Thanks, but that won't be enough. I'm sure Mrs. Russo won't give an inch," she said, biting her lip.

Dax took both her hands in his. "Look, why stay in New York? If you're losing your loft anyway, why not move to Red Rock? You've been running things by fax and phone. Why not continue this way indefinitely? Red Rock would be an economical alternative."

She shook her head. "There are inexpensive places all over the country."

"I just thought Red Rock might have a little more appeal than most places," he said, his voice low, almost quiet.

"This is a business decision, Dax. You've got business reasons for making the decisions you make, it's only fair that I do the same."

"So what happens now?" he asked.

"I had a handshake agreement with you. I'll honor it, of course," she replied.

Dax agonized. "I feel like I've let you down."

She shook her head. "You'd have helped if you could, I know that." She looked at her watch. "I'd better get over to Ford's and take care of the formalities."

He took her hands again, this time squeezing them tight. "Will you have dinner with me tonight?"

"I don't think so. Let's let last night be our goodbye. That's better, don't you think?" she said.

"I don't like the sound of goodbye."

Chloe smiled weakly. "You're not sounding like a levelheaded businessman, Dax. You've done fine to this point, keep your eye on the ball."

"Please, don't talk that way," he said.

She blinked back a tear. "I meant it as a compliment. Honest. I really did."

Without another word, Chloe slipped from the booth and headed for the front of the club. Dax watched her go, knowing things were going from bad to worse. But what could he do? He couldn't force her to stay in Red Rock, not if New York and her business was more important than anything he had to offer.

CHLOE STEPPED OUT into the afternoon sun just as Heath Barnett came hurrying up to the door.

"Hi, Chloe," he said, tipping his hat. "Understand you're leavin' us."

"That's right," she said with a sigh, her insides still shaky. "My flight's tomorrow."

"To be honest, I'm surprised Dax is letting you go. Word around town is that he's pretty damn fond of you."

"Is that right?"

Heath stared down at his feet, embarrassed. "Maybe I'm speaking out of turn saying that, but it's hardly a secret."

"Well, not all rumors are true. But I don't mean to keep you, Heath," she said. "You looked like you were in a hurry."

"I am." He glanced at his watch. "I've got to get a check from Dax and take it over to the bank."

Chloe's eyebrows rose. "Oh?"

"Yeah. We're doing an investment together. Cattle futures. Don't suppose it'll hurt telling you, considering you're leaving town. Not that it's all that much of a secret. When our two hundred grand becomes half a mil in a month or so, the whole town will hear about it anyway."

Her jaw dropped. "You and Dax are investing two hundred thousand dollars in cattle?"

"Cattle futures. This fella I know who really has a grip on the market called me this morning and said, 'It's time for you boys to get out your checkbooks.' So I gave Dax the high sign."

"Dax must be investing a token amount."

Heath shifted uneasily. "I see I should have kept my mouth shut. I've been so excited all day, I can hardly keep from blabbing. Do me a favor, will you, Chloe, and forget we had this conversation?"

"Sure, Heath. But under one condition. Tell me Dax is not an equal partner in this cattle futures deal."

"Actually, Chloe, he *is* an equal partner. Fifty-fifty."

Her heart dropped into her stomach. "Dax is about to give you a hundred thousand dollars?"

He winced. "Me and my big mouth."

"Don't worry, I won't tell a soul. But please do me a favor, Heath. Tell him that I wish him every success with his investment and that I hope he becomes a very rich man."

Heath tipped his hat and she turned and walked away. Tears stung her eyes as she hurried across the street to Ford's office. She was going to sign those papers, pack her things and be on her way to Denver before Mr. Dax Charboneau could get his hundred-thousand-dollar check in Heath's hand. And she wasn't going to look back. Ever.

13

BY THE TIME her plane landed in New York, Chloe thought she had it all figured out—she would throw herself into her work, use every spare moment to search for new quarters for her operation and she would never, ever, date anyone she was doing business with again.

But even as she made that resolution, Chloe knew in her heart of hearts that Angela had been right. The problem wasn't that she and Dax had been partners in the Cowboy Club, or that he'd betrayed her. The real issue was Dax himself. The man didn't have a clue when it came to wanting to share his life. Oh, he'd share an evening with a willing lady, but he didn't even understand why Clay would want to marry Erica. And if he couldn't figure that one out, the chances of his ever feeling the need to have a family of his own were nil.

Chloe went to her parents' house for Sunday dinner after she returned home. She was still hurting, and badly wanted to talk things over with her mother. When her father sat down in front of the television to root for the Yankees, Chloe joined Martine in the kitchen. As her mother grated cheese for a quiche, Chloe poured her heart out to her.

"But *chérie*," Martine said when she had finished the tale, "don't you know that in every woman's life there is one man, one special man, who takes her heart and breaks it? Love is like that sometimes. But life goes on. Trust me, Chloe, you will love again. There is so much love in you, and someday the right man will see that."

She hugged her mother, grateful for her wisdom and support. But Martine's words didn't make the emptiness go away. Chloe had a feeling that wouldn't change for a long time.

During dinner that evening, the three of them discussed what she should do about finding a new location for her business. Her father offered to let her use one of his shops. He had been trying to sell the smallest one for months.

"That's very generous, Dad, but if you hang on long enough, you might find a buyer. You and Mother need that money for your retirement. Besides, the place is too small for my needs. I'd still have to get an apartment, and it would be too far for Carlo and Donatella to commute, so they'd have to move, too."

"But what will you do if you can't find anything affordable? Rents are sky high these days. Are you prepared to leave New York?"

Chloe had been shocked that her father would even suggest such a thing. "How could I? Carlo and Donatella wouldn't want to leave here. And it'd take me forever to find anyone to replace them." She pinched his cheek. "Besides, Dad, if I moved, who would tell you that the Mets are really a much better team than the Yankees?"

Her father put down his fork. His expression was serious. "I may not be rooting for the Yankees much longer anyway." He looked at his wife, who nodded. "Your mother and I have been thinking about moving. The doctor agrees with her that I should cut back. If we sold all three shops and left New York, we'd do okay. The main reason we haven't wanted to go before now was you."

Martine nodded. "Perhaps, Chloe, if you can't find anything in your price range here, then we could all move together."

"Where were you thinking of going?" she asked.

Martine smiled. "Your father says Florida. I think California. The wine country, it is very much like France, very chic. It would be close to San Francisco, too."

Chloe was dumbfounded. "How long have you been considering this?"

"For a while now," her father said. "Your mother has been after me to retire ever since my heart attack, you know."

"Well, to tell you the truth, I think New York is the best place for my business. My first choice would be to stay. But at the same time, I don't want you two to hang on here if you're ready to move elsewhere."

They didn't say any more about it—Chloe knew that anything her parents did was a long way off since they would have to sell their home as well as all three repair shops before they could move. But the conversation made enough of an impression on her that she posed a hypothetical question to Carlo and Donatella the next day.

"If I can't find anything suitable here, what would the two of you think about moving away from New York?"

Carlo shrugged his shoulders. "I don't know. We left Italy because we wanted to see the world and so far we've only seen New York. So, depending on where you went, it would be okay with me. What do you think, Donatella?"

The brunette with the merry brown eyes smiled. "We will move to Arizona or California when we retire. If we leave here ten years early, what difference would it make?''

Chloe was relieved, because it gave her some options. In fact, she thought about options and choices a lot the following two days as she met with real estate leasing agents and looked over prospective work space. When she wasn't searching for a new home for her business, she met with the relatives of the Kuwaiti princess and took the largest order she had ever gotten.

Then, two things happened that put her in a funk. First, she got a phone call from a client in Chicago. Chloe had faxed her the sketch of the hand-tooled cordovan leather shoes that had been inspired by the cowgirl boots in Red Rock. The woman called to say she loved them and wanted more ''western-looking'' shoes. Chloe promised to come up with another design. But though she was grateful for the sale, she wasn't thrilled with the reminder.

Second, when the mail came, she was reminded of Red Rock again when she got an invitation to Clay and Erica's wedding. Chloe sent them a lovely note, telling them she wouldn't be able to return for the ceremony.

But the invitation brought back so many memories. Not only of Dax, but of all the good friends she had made in Red Rock. Jamie would officiate at their wedding, maybe even wearing the new black shoes she'd ordered if Carlo finished them in time. Wanda would be there in her sandals, along with Julia. And of course, Wiley, Ford, Heath, Quentin Starr and Dax.

Chloe sighed. At last she understood what Jamie had been trying to tell her about the Cowboy Club. There *was* magic in the place. It had worked on her, made her fall in love with a whole town, in a way. It was just too damn bad that it hadn't worked its magic on Dax.

CHLOE PICKED UP her glass and took a sip of wine as she looked around the room at her friends. For the first time since she'd become a member of the Thursday Night Club for Divorcées, Spinsters and Other Reprobates, she hadn't wanted to come to the meeting. Not that she didn't want to see her friends, but as she'd told Angela on the telephone the night before, it wouldn't be pleasant telling the tale of Red Rock.

"Hey, kiddo, we're your friends through thick and thin. Besides, there isn't a one of us, even Ariel, who hasn't been hurt at least once. Everyone will understand."

So she had come, and she had told everyone the gory details about her adventures out West.

"So," Ariel said, "the bottom line is that Mr. Wonderful let you get away. What a fool."

"Hear, hear," Angela said. "I'll second that."

"Me, too," Wendy chimed in. "But the worst part of it is that he didn't help you when you needed it."

Chloe shook her head. "Oh, that's not fair. I was real upset at the time, but Dax and I had made a deal and I shouldn't have tried to change it. His sin was in not being honest with me. He should have said straight out that he wanted to stick to our deal, not give me a song and dance about not having the cash."

"What will you do now? Have you found another location?" Ariel asked.

Chloe shook her head. "No, nothing wonderful yet."

"Then what will you do?" Sharon asked.

"I don't know," she said, pasting a brave smile on her face. "But I'm a whole lot better off financially now." Chloe cleared her throat. "Enough about me, though. I want to hear what the rest of you have been up to while I was away."

"Sharon's got a new boyfriend," Ariel purred in a singsong voice.

Chloe turned to the brunette, noting an extra sparkle in Sharon's chocolate brown eyes. "Come on. Tell all."

"Well, he's not *exactly* a boyfriend," Sharon began, giggling. "More like a…well…a Mr. Tonight who has turned into a Mr. Man-of-the-Month."

Chuckling, Chloe said, "I'm sure there's one hell of a good story behind that. Want to clue me in, or has everyone else heard the details so many times that they'd be bored to death?"

"Heavens, Chloe, you know we're never bored with a good war story," Angela said.

"Gosh, no," Wendy agreed. "Things have been so dry in my neck of the woods that living vicariously is all I've got anyway."

"What about your memories?" Ariel, the former model, suggested.

Wendy shot her a dirty look. "I'm tired of those. They're starting to get like a rerun of the movie of the week I've seen too many times." She picked up her glass and took a healthy slug of wine. "What I need is fresh meat…"

Everyone hooted.

"If not of the real variety, at least of the second-hand kind," she continued.

Rubbing her hands together gleefully, Sharon grinned. "Well, if that's the case, I'll be glad to oblige."

With that, Sharon Walton launched into her latest escapades. Chloe tried to pay attention, and she made sure to laugh at the appropriate places. But part of her wondered if this was all there was—talking about men who never turned out to be as wonderful as you'd hoped. Sure, once in a while one of them, like Belinda, found true love. But for the most part it was hit-and-miss, with more misses than hits.

That had been okay with her before she'd gone to Red Rock, because finding a soul mate hadn't been a high priority. Dax had changed all that. He'd shown her what it was like to be with someone who understood the way you were, deep down. Not that it had done any good, because when push came to shove, his priorities had not made room for her needs. And that was so sad.

Of course, he'd given her no good reason to expect that it would be any different. The only problem was, knowing it didn't seem to make the pain go away. Nothing did.

BY THE TIME Chloe got back to her loft, she was exhausted. Instead of concentrating on business and spending the day designing shoes for the cousins of the Kuwaiti princess, she had pounded the pavement, looking for a new workshop. She had met with leasing agents and scoured ads in the paper. In three weeks she'd have to move out of the loft, and that wasn't nearly enough time. What to do? What to do?

She opened the big wire cage on the freight elevator that led to the loft entrance and dug into her purse for her key. As she did, a flicker of movement caught her eye. A man was sitting on the floor at the end of the hallway. A black cowboy hat was pulled down over his face, as if he was asleep. As she put the key in the lock, and he took off his hat, she saw that it was Dax.

Chloe's heart lurched but she didn't say a word as he got to his feet. He was wearing jeans, a black turtleneck and a black sport coat. If it weren't for the hat and boots, he'd have almost looked like a New Yorker. Oddly, he was carrying a briefcase.

"Dax, what are you doing here?"

"Just happened to be in the neighborhood and thought I'd say hi."

"No, I'm serious. What are you doing in New York?"

"I know it's late, Chloe, but can I come in for a few minutes? I've come a long way and I need to speak with you. It's business."

Her first impulse was to say no. She'd heard it all before—both the excuses and the lies—and she didn't want to go through it again, no matter what he had to say. But she realized that would be childish. Dax wouldn't have come unless he'd thought it was important. She'd give him the time of day. Be polite. Fair. And *then* she'd ask him to leave.

She unlocked the door before she answered. "Will this take long? I'm bushed and I have an early appointment with a leasing agent."

"No. I'll say my piece and get out of your hair."

She nodded curtly and went inside, turning on the overhead lights. Dax followed, craning his neck to look at the shelf after shelf of colorful fabrics and leathers that spilled from floor to ceiling. Chloe watched him, taking in the way his jeans hugged his thighs and buns. She started to recall how those thighs had felt pressed against her when they were making love, but then she forced herself to remember that was in the past. She had to stay focused. Dax had said he was here on business.

"Come on back to the living area," she said, leading the way. She headed straight for the kitchen and, as she walked, she heard the hollow sound of Dax's cowboy boots on the hardwood floors. She indicated that he could sit on a bar stool, facing the kitchen, then she went to the refrigerator. "Can I offer you anything to drink?"

"I'm fine," he said, setting his briefcase on the counter.

"Well, if you don't mind, I'm going to have some apple juice." Chloe set the bottle on the counter. When she reached up to get a glass from the cabinet, she felt Dax's eyes on her. But she couldn't react to that…she wouldn't let herself.

She carefully poured herself some juice. Then, after putting the bottle back in the fridge, she turned to him. "I believe you said you wanted to discuss business," she prompted.

He nodded. "Yes. I want you to design some cowboy boots. For me."

She opened her mouth to speak but nothing came out. Nothing! A thousand thoughts streamed through her mind. *Cowboy boots! After all they'd gone through, he came here because he wanted a pair of cowboy boots! What could he be thinking? Had he gone mad?* But instead of voicing them, she took a sip of juice and calmly said, "Sorry. I don't do men's boots. Cowboy or otherwise."

He leaned forward, his manner earnest. "But you could, couldn't you? I mean, that's what you're in business for. And I know you do men's shoes because you said you made shoes for your dad."

She drew in a deep breath. "Oh, yes. From a technical standpoint I could do as you ask. It's a matter of…shall we say, interest? Interest in the project."

"And you aren't interested?" he asked flatly.

She shook her head.

"Even for the right price?"

She set down her juice and crossed her arms.

"Why are you here, Dax? Please, just spit it out because I don't want to play games."

"I want cowboy boots. Black ones. A handmade pair and I want you to design and make them. And I'm prepared to pay for the privilege."

"Anything wrong with your present boots?"

"Nope."

"Then…"

"No games, Chloe. I just want you to make the boots. Call it a souvenir if you want." He put his briefcase on the counter of the bar separating the kitchen from the living-room area. "You see, I came here to balance the books."

Chloe blinked. "And you think the way to do that is to order a pair of cowboy boots?"

"Yes. In return, I'm prepared to pay you a handsome price. Very handsome."

"How handsome?"

He opened his briefcase and took out several papers. "I know you might find this hard to believe, but I want to make it up to you for letting you down…"

She rolled her eyes.

"No. Please hear me out."

"All right," she said. "Common courtesy says you deserve that much. But if this is going to take more than five minutes, let's go to the living room."

Dax got off the bar stool and went to the white duck couch. He sat down, putting his papers on the glass and brass coffee table. Chloe sat down next to him, but at a safe distance.

"First, I know you're worried about finding a new place to work and live. You said you were meeting with a leasing agent tomorrow, so can I assume you haven't found anyplace suitable yet?"

"Correct."

"Well, I may be able to help with that." He handed

her a sheaf of papers. "This is an option to buy the loft. I spoke with Mrs. Russo's cousin, Emile, and he's willing to let you remain here three more months at your present rent. At the end of that time, you can either move out or buy this place for the terms originally outlined by Mrs. Russo."

She glanced down at the papers, flabbergasted. "Dax, how…why would you…what are you doing talking to Mrs. Russo's cousin, anyway?"

"Let's just say I took matters into my own hands."

She paused to process that. "Why would Emile let me stay here for an additional three months?"

"I made it worth his while."

"What do you mean by that?"

"I found a way to make it work. The rest is up to you."

"I'd still have to come up with a hundred thousand dollars in cash," Chloe said. "And that's a little over ninety-five thousand dollars more than the check you're supposed to send me this month."

"I know. But I can help with that, too. I'm prepared to restructure our deal on the Cowboy Club so that you'll have more cash."

A thousand questions came to her. She wanted to know what had caused the change of heart, not to mention the change of circumstances. But the only words that came to her were, "Why now?"

"Because I finally figured out a way to help you. You came to me that last morning, asking for help…"

"And you said you couldn't help me."

She watched as he took a deep, fortifying breath. "I was telling the truth, Chloe. I'd made a commitment to Heath Barnett and Morgan Prescott months earlier and that hundred thousand was earmarked for the cattle futures deal." He paused dramatically. "It's also true that I would have backed out of that deal if it was the only possible way to buy out your interest in the Cowboy Club."

"But you didn't tell me that." It was a struggle, but she managed to keep her voice low and even.

"No. Just as you didn't tell me that you'd be willing to sell out for as little as a quarter of a million. We both wanted the best deal possible."

"All right," Chloe said. "I can see that. Bottom line is that you had your priorities and I had mine. But why the sudden desire to help? Or are you telling me that you've already made a killing in the cattle futures market and now you want to help me to ease your conscience?"

Dax reached over and took her hand. Chloe wanted to pull it away, but when she felt the warmth of his skin against her, she couldn't. For the life of her, she couldn't. So instead, she looked into Dax's eyes and waited.

"I do want to help you," he said, "if you'll let me." He absently rubbed the back of her hand with his thumb. It brought back many good memories, but she didn't want to respond to that, so she forced herself not to react. "And no, I haven't made a killing in the market. Not yet. But I did sell my house."

She was stunned. Dax loved his house. She remembered him telling her that owning a home had been extra special to him because he'd grown up in an orphanage. He'd even waited to build it until he could do so without getting a mortgage. "But why? You loved your house."

"It didn't feel right anymore," he said, scooting closer. "Not without you. After I'd seen what it was like to share it, I couldn't abide the thought of being alone on my own patio, or making breakfast just for me, or sleeping alone in that bed."

His words touched her heart, but she also knew

that didn't necessarily mean they belonged together. Sure, they'd shared a lot. But it wasn't written anywhere that would lead to the kind of commitment she'd probably want sooner or later.

"So, you're saying you sold your house because it didn't feel right without me? Is that it?"

"And also because it gave me the cash I needed to help you with your problem. Quentin Starr decided to stay in Red Rock and he didn't want to wait to build a home. He offered me a good price for the place, lock, stock and barrel, all cash, if I'd clear out in ten days. So I cut a deal with Jamie to rent Cody's place, packed my bags and took my check from Quentin. I came here as soon as I could."

She sighed. "So now we're both in the same boat. Homeless."

"I wouldn't go quite that far. Thanks to Emile seeing reason, you've got three more months here. Then you'll have to decide whether to buy this place or not." He touched her cheek with the back of his hand.

"And why wouldn't I want to stay here? New York is my home," she added, ignoring the fact that his thigh was right next to hers. She could feel the warmth of it through his jeans.

"Because you might decide that being in Red Rock is a better deal."

She swallowed hard, almost afraid to say the words. "How so?"

"Well, if you want, you could relocate your business and run it out of the saddlery. I'd either sell you the building or rent it to you, at your option."

"I see. And the three months is to decide which alternative I want, New York or Red Rock?"

"Yes. And it's also time to discover whether or not you want me."

She felt her heart skip a beat, but still, she held herself in check. She didn't want to be let down again. It hurt too much. "What, exactly, are you offering?"

"Chloe, I know it's been fast, but we found something special with each other. I told you once that when I came to Red Rock it felt right to me—like home. And after you left, I realized that's how I felt about you, too." He paused, looking into her eyes. "I know it took me a while to understand, but I've never had a family before. I never wanted one until I met you. But we have something that I don't want to let go of. And I'm willing to do what it takes to find out if we can make it work permanently. That may mean my staying here in New York—"

"You'd be willing to do that?"

He nodded. "If that's what it took. But my first choice is for us to return to Red Rock. I'd like to keep the Cowboy Club and have you run your business from there. But first, I've got to square things with you." He took a deep breath and continued. "With three more months here, you'll have time to decide if we belong together. If we both feel we do, then the only question is if it's here or out West. Either way, I'll restructure our deal on the Cowboy Club. You'll have the cash you need to do whatever you want."

"And how do you propose we spend the next three months? Do you stay here?"

"That's up to you. But I'd like us to go back to Red Rock for Clay and Erica's wedding. If you want to spend more time there, good. Maybe you can even help me find a piece of land to build a new house."

She arched an eyebrow. "And if it doesn't work out between us…what then? What do you get for your trouble, Dax?"

"I guess just a pair of boots."

Chloe laughed. Really laughed. Dax must have understood that she'd finally let down her guard because he pulled her onto his lap and kissed her hard. And when she finally came up for air, Dax looked deep into her eyes and said, "I love you, Chloe. And dammit, I don't like this idea of us being two thousand miles apart."

She sighed. Then, tracing his lower lip with her finger, she said, "I love you, too. But I knew from the first you'd be trouble."

"Then isn't it fortunate that you're the kind of woman who can handle trouble?"

She smiled. "Dax, I'll be satisfied if I can learn to handle you."

But he didn't answer her. Instead, he kissed her again.

Epilogue

WILEY COOPER LEANED back in his office chair as he reviewed the lead story for the next edition of the *Red Rock Recorder*. He was putting the paper to bed tonight and it was a darn good thing, too, because it had been a long day. The Charboneau wedding had taken place that morning in the community church and Jamie had officiated. Then there'd been a huge reception at the Cowboy Club afterward. The bride's parents and a whole passel of her friends had come from New York City for the event.

Wiley glanced at his watch. He still had half an hour to fiddle with his story and come up with a headline before he was going to meet his friends at the Cowboy Club for a nightcap. Not that they hadn't gotten their fill of champagne at the wedding reception, but that had been hours ago. By now Dax and Chloe were well on their way to New Orleans. And Wiley was still wrangling with a few final details.

Any way he cut it, Dax Charboneau marrying Chloe James had been a story worth printing. But the fact that his friend had finally met his match made the story front-page news. Besides, it was the most noteworthy thing that had happened in Red Rock— at least this week.

Wiley sighed. He still hadn't figured out the headline. He'd gotten Julia to help him with a description of the wedding dress—an off-white bustier, laced in front, over a balloon skirt. The hat Chloe wore had ostrich plumes and sinamay, some sort of tulle. At least, that's what the women called it. For his money, it had looked like an old-fashioned dress, something from the Old West, which made it an odd choice, considering that the bride was from New York. But then Wanda had insisted that was Chloe's tribute to Red Rock, her way of showing that she fit in.

Maybe. He wouldn't know about things like that. All he could say for sure was that her boots had darn near stolen the show. Every woman at the wedding had raved about them. Hell, even Julia had claimed that they were so stunning she simply had to have a pair like them. And he had to admit, it had surprised him that the little lady from New York City had gotten married in a pair of cream and gold Old West–style boots.

Wiley snapped his fingers. That was it! His headline! *THE BRIDE WORE BOOTS!*

Welcome Back to

THE COWBOY CLUB

The romance and fun continues in
July 1999 with the third book
in this exciting new miniseries,
The Cowboy Club, by bestselling
author Janice Kaiser.

Here's a sample of what's to come in

#737 *The Baby and the Cowboy*

WILEY COOPER got off the barstool and moved closer to the window, so that he could peer down the street in both directions. There was no sign of Jessica Kilmer. He shook his head, amused with himself. One date with the lady and she'd sure as shootin' gotten under his skin. Hell, he was as nervous as a teenage boy on prom night, waiting for her return to Red Rock.

He looked at his watch again, then cocked his head when he thought he heard something. "You guys hear that?"

"What?" Dax said.

"That sound. A kind of gurgling."

They were all quiet for a moment but there was silence. Wiley rubbed his neck. "I must be tired. I'm hearing things."

"Why not go on home?" Dax urged. "I'll wait here with Ford."

"Oh no. I don't mind," Wiley said, a shade too quickly. Again he saw Dax look at him, but this time there was a smile on his face. Wiley was sure he suspected exactly how taken he was with the lovely lawyer from Texas.

There was another sound, louder this time. "There it is again," Wiley said.

Ford got off his barstool, suddenly alert. All three men stood at the entrance of the Cowboy Club, close to where Wanda stationed herself to greet customers.

Wiley glanced behind the podium where she kept the reservation book but didn't see anything. Then he heard a sound coming from the vestibule. Dax opened the first set of doors. It was dark, but with the street lamps they were able to see light through the swinging bar doors that accessed the wooden sidewalk.

At first Wiley didn't see anything unusual. But then, when he looked down, he spotted a large basket in the corner. He stepped close to get a better look just as Dax flipped the light switch. Wiley blanched. Somebody had left a baby at the Cowboy Club!

"Jumpin Jeosophat, where'd that come from?" Ford exclaimed as he leaned past Wiley to take a look.

"Not the stork, that's for sure," Wiley said, picking up the basket. He stepped through the swinging bar doors and peered up and down the street. It was empty. He glanced down at the baby, who was dressed in a little blue shirt with cowboy boots on it—a boy. He was waving his arms and gurgling. There was a note pinned to his shirt. There were also some jars of food and a bottle and some extra diapers.

"See anyone?" Dax asked.

"Not a soul." Wiley turned to take the baby back inside. Dax kept the door open for him and he set the basket on the bar and unpinned the note, which he handed to Ford. "You're the mayor, so I guess you should read this."

Ford looked kind of shell-shocked, but he reached into his vest pocket and pulled out his reading glasses. "What the hell is going on?" he mumbled.

Wiley turned his attention to the baby, reaching out to touch his waving hand. When the baby grabbed onto his finger and cooed, Wiley was flooded with a thousand memories of his daughter Shelly. She'd waved her arms and legs a lot, too. His ex-wife Joyce had tried to tell him that all babies did that but Wiley hadn't believed her. He was certain that Shelly was letting him know how happy she was to see him.

Ford harrumphed as he read the note. His eyebrows shot up and he gave Wiley a funny look. Then he silently passed the piece of paper to Dax. Dax whistled, and looked askance at Wiley, then handed him the note.

Dear Mr. Cooper,

Hi! My name is Nathaniel Gordon Springer and I'm nine months old. I'm real sorry to meet you like this, but my mother is hoping that you'll find a place in your heart for me. My grandpa was Lucas Springer, and if he was still alive, I know he'd take care of me. But he's gone now, and my mom can't take care of me any longer. She wants you to know that she tried real hard to do the right thing, just like her daddy taught her, but she just couldn't make enough money to feed me and give me the life she wants me to have.

I want to grow up in Red Rock on the Double C, like she did. Since you're alone, she thought you might like me for company. I'll try hard to be a good little boy if you'll adopt me and raise me as your son. You won't regret it.

Please don't turn me away.

Love,
Nathaniel

P.S. My favorite food is applesauce.

He looked up from the note. The baby—Nathaniel—was still gurgling. Wiley took in the big blue eyes and blonde hair. The kid looked like Lucas, all right. Wiley took a deep breath, feeling as if someone had kicked him in the stomach. He thought of Sally Anne, Lucas's little girl. He'd called her Sally Sunshine. She'd been sweet and loving, and he'd always considered her a second daughter. It had about killed him when he'd had to deliver the news that her father was dead—and all because of him. Even now, Wiley remembered how she'd stared at him with those huge blue eyes of hers, willing him to tell her it wasn't true, that it was some kind of joke.

He looked up at Ford and Dax. The mayor spoke first. "When's the last time you heard from Maggie and Sally Anne?"

"Nearly two years ago. Sally Anne wrote to me, asking for a loan. I could tell that Maggie had dictated the letter. I sent them a couple of grand." He slowly exhaled. "If this is Sally Anne's kid, something awful must have happened. She wasn't the type to get into trouble."

Ford nodded. "I agree. The question is what we do now? Abandoning a baby is a crime. We'll have to locate Sally Anne, and she's going to have to face the consequences. But even more urgent, we'll have to find someone to care for this baby. It's nearly midnight. Too late to contact anyone in Cortez with the child protective services." He scratched his ear. "I'll have to make a few calls in the morning to find out what the procedure is."

"But what about tonight?" Dax said.

Ford looked at him. "Can't you and Chloe take him in? It's only until tomorrow. Besides, the kid was left at the Cowboy Club and, well, you're the owner…"

Dax shook his head. "I don't think that means Sally Anne wants the kid to grow up in a bar, Ford, but nice try. Besides, we can't take him in because Chloe has a sore throat. We can't risk letting him get sick. How about the sheriff? Shouldn't he be responsible?"

"Don't know if you heard," Wiley said, "but Bryant went to the hospital this afternoon with a ruptured appendix."

Dax turned to Ford. "You're the mayor. As the only official around, it should be your responsibility."

"Me!" he exclaimed. "I'm an old bachelor. What would I do with a baby?"

Wiley rolled his eyes.

Ford took a deep breath, obviously trying to come up with a better argument. "Wiley, it's clear from the note that Sally Anne wants you to raise the boy. I know there's no way that's going to happen, but in a moral sense, it *is* your problem. So I hereby appoint you to be in charge of the baby's welfare for tonight."

Nathaniel squealed. All three men turned to look at him. The baby was gurgling and waving his arms and legs like crazy.

Ford grinned ear to ear and slapped Wiley on the back. "I think that means the baby agrees with me. Congratulations, Wiley. You're a father again!"

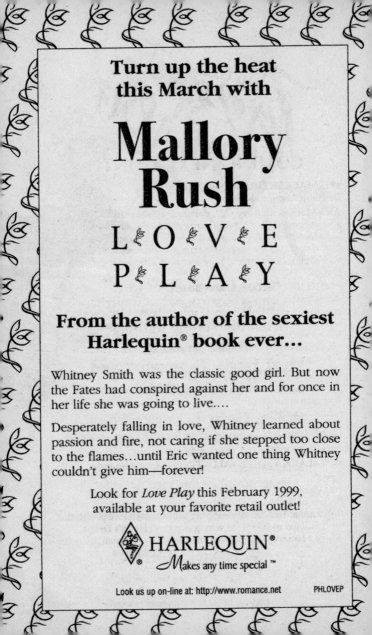

COMING NEXT MONTH